Chris Nickson was born and raised in America for 30 years, working as a mus more than 30 non-fiction books, he retu days he's best known for his historical crime novels, including the Richard Nottingham series, set in Leeds in the 1730s, the Tom Harper books, which take place in late Victorian Leeds, and the 1950s noir *Dark Briggate Blues*.

Leeds, the Biography

A History of Leeds in Short Stories

Chris Nickson

Published by Armley Press 2015

Cover Design:

Author cover photo by

Layout: Ian Dobson

ISBN 0-9554699-?-?

Contents

Introduction

Every city, every town, every village has a history that goes as deep as the country itself. It's a glorious web that stretches across time. But all too often, the only thing most people know of history is dates and Acts of Parliament, and they only tell one small fragment of the story.

History is about people. Not just those deemed the great and the good, but ordinary folk, too. Many of them have no memorials, or at best a fleeting mention, like Alice Musgrave, the first girl diagnosed in the Leeds plague outbreak of 1645.

What happens in these stories is fiction, of course, but it's really an attempt to put a very human face on the history of Leeds from 363 CE up to 1963. While some important figures from the past are there – there have to be references to the merchant and philanthropist John Harrison, painter J. Atkinson Grimshaw, and the first great historian of Leeds, Ralph Thoresby – this is a lens that mostly looks at the people who have been lost in time. It's as close as many will come to a headstone, and it's something they deserve.

Awful things have happened in Leeds – Cambodunum, as the Romans perhaps named it. There was the Harrying of the North by William the Conqueror, and the ways the poor were so often brutally treated through time are very real, lying just at the edge of memory. All I've done is give a voice to the victims. But there have been wonderful moments, too – the building of Briggate eight centuries ago, the museum that Thoresby accumulated, the Battle of Holbeck Moor. Whether good or bad, they're all shadings in a tale that stretches back over centuries, and one that will continue for many years to come.

Leeds hasn't been kind to its past. Walk around the centre and you'll see plenty of grand Victorian buildings, testament to the prosperity and pride of a time when Leeds was booming (for some) and there was a sense of greatness here. Try to go back further, however, and there's very little. A few pubs, a couple of churches, and the gable end of a house. That's not a great deal.

Leeds made its fortune and its name on the wool trade. First by the buying and selling in the markets every Tuesday and Saturday, then in the production of off-the-peg suits. It's a history that's long gone now, but we shouldn't forget it.

And we're a city of immigrants. Remember that Leeds – Loidis as it was known then – was once part of the Danelaw; many of the street names come from the Norse language. And they arrived after the Saxons, the Romans, and others. Some from each wave settled here, took wives and raised families. Later, people arrived in the town from the country, hoping to find the streets paved with gold. Then, in the middle of the 19th century, the Irish came, followed by the Jews, and half a century later, West Indians, Indians, and Pakistanis, followed and after them people from all over the world. The newcomers in the poor neighbourhoods that the previous new arrivals had vacated as they began to earn a little money. They renew us and start a fresh cycle.

Not every landmark event is here. If anyone reads this and wants to know more about the events that shaped the city, there are plenty of excellent books out there, and the Thoresby Society, as well as Leeds Library and Leeds Central Library can point people in the right direction. The choices here are purely personal.

The history of Leeds is the history of everyone who's ever lived here, whether great or small. The people are the core of it all. This is a tribute to them, an attempt to have them live and breathe again, to let us all see what went before.

Widow's Weeds – 360CE

'I don't see why they need a coffin, anyway,' Bellator said. 'From what I heard, there wasn't enough of him left to be worth burying.'

The cart moved slowly along the rutted tracks, branches rubbing along the sides as the ox plodded on. It had taken the best part of two hours to load the stone coffin and lid, and with each dip and lurch it seemed as if the axle would break.

'Their choice,' Lucillus told him with a shrug. He was a heavy man, somewhere around thirty, his knuckles covered with scars, a thick, ruddy beard on his cheeks. He reached for the wineskin under the seat and took a drink. 'They paid good money for it. It's the Christian way, they say, put them in the ground so they can go to heaven.' He'd been the one who'd done all the work, chipping away at the rock until there was room for the head and body, just like any other coffin, then shaping the lid. Bellator was just the carter.

A hot gust of wind burst out of the west and scoured their faces. Summer, Lucillus thought wryly. That was the way it had been this year. Usually even prayer couldn't keep the rains away. But it had been dry since early spring, the grass brown and dead, dust kicking up and choking the throat whenever a man walked.

'Almost there now,' the driver said. 'It's well before the road to Eboracum.' He shifted on the seat, big belly rolling, and used the goad on the ox. It didn't seem to make any difference; the animal wouldn't move any faster.

Lucillus had never come this far north before. The settlement was just south of the river, a cluster of twelve houses around the stone ford. When he ventured out, it was usually into country he knew so well he could almost travel it in his sleep. He felt safer there, where family and friends were close. Troops had come to Cambodunum three times in his life, once a whole century of them, exotic men babbling away in languages he didn't understand as they pitched their tents overnight, buying food and drink. Next morning they left so early that they could have been figures from a dream. When the order for the coffin came, he'd been taken by surprise. He worked a little with stone when he wasn't trying to grow crops. And with this weather they wouldn't grow. The pay for the job was too good to refuse; it would keep them going for two months, himself, his wife and their two children.

Bellator turned on to a smaller track, hardly wide enough for the cart.

'They're a strange family,' he said. 'Done well for themselves, selling to the garrison over at Adel and the soldiers up in Eboracum. I don't know what they'll do now he's dead, though. I can't see her running the business and the son isn't old enough yet.' He leaned over the side and spat.

It had taken a pair of slaves most of yesterday to dig the grave. Under the topsoil the earth was hard as iron. Out in the field the crops were all withered and hopeless, and bones showed through the flesh of the cattle that milled around, snuffling around hungrily for food. Not that there was any to give them. At this time of year they should have been able to crop the lush, dark grass. But what little remained was dry, brittle, with no nourishment at all.

She'd looked at the accounts her husband had kept on long rolls, taking out a wax tablet and spending hours over the calculations. There were coins in the chest, but half of those were owed, bills that needed to be paid soon. Without a good harvest and fair prices for the cattle they wouldn't be able to see out another winter here.

He might have had an answer. He always seemed to have the answer, using his charm to arrange a loan here, to haggle down a price there, and leaving the other person feeling he'd done them a favour. It was a strange talent, she thought, but he'd used it well. They'd prospered, moving from farmhouse to a villa as grand as any Roman official. And then he had to let himself be killed by a boar. Killed and torn apart so that all they'd managed to a find was a leg and half an arm, hand still clutching a spear.

'Mama?'

Vassura turned away from the window to face her son. Morirex looked so much like his father that it made her heart ache every time she saw him. But where Glevo had always seemed so assured, in control of everything, the boy had all the uncertainty of youth. Still, he was thirteen, what could she expect from him?

'What is it, sweetheart?' She kept her voice tender and smiled at him.

'The men are here with the coffin,' he told her, in the voice that had deepened just a season before.

She'd heard them arrive, the harsh squeak of an axle that desperately needed greasing and the shout of the carter.

'I'll be out in a moment. Give them a cup of wine and

gather the men.'

'Yes, mama.'

Alone, she wandered through the room, touching every object she passed as if bidding each one farewell. In a way she was, Vassura thought. A farewell to him. He'd be under the ground very soon, ready to meet his god.

The way Glevo had embraced the new religion had always seemed strange to her. But he'd seen it as the future; that was what he'd said. He'd found something in it that eluded her. She was content enough with her small household gods and an offering in the stream at the bottom of the valley each spring. At least he'd never mocked her for what she believed, little as it was. He'd been a good husband and father.

Just stupid at times. Why he'd gone after the boar on his own she couldn't understand. In the past he'd always taken at least two slaves with him when he hunted, men he trusted. This time, though, he'd left soon after dawn, certain he'd be back well before sunset with meat for them all. It was as if he'd wanted to prove himself in some way. Instead they hadn't found him until the following day, after the wolves had taken everything of him they wanted. The men had brought the remains home in a sack, reluctant to show her until she'd insisted.

She'd kept her tears until she was alone, cold and rigid as a corpse herself in bed. She'd forced herself to wait, not to show all the turmoil that filled her; the children needed to see her strong. Morirex had been uncertain what he should do, whether to cry like a child or become the man of the house, firm and unemotional. Narina had wept. She was eight, no more than a girl still, and the world swept over her at the loss of her father.

'We'll ease it down there,' Lucillus said. The four slaves looked at him doubtfully. He'd arranged two stout boards going from the back of the cart to the ground. Together they could manage it; after all, they'd been able to put it *in* the cart. He glanced at Bellator. The carter shrugged and took a sip of the wine the boy from the house had offered.

Lucillus pushed the men into place then climbed into the cart.

'Right,' he ordered. 'Pull and take the weight as it starts to move.' Very slowly the coffin began to shift. At first it seemed as if they'd never succeed, then, as the sweat started to pour down their faces, it scraped over the wood, sliding along over the boards until it touched the earth. 'Pull it!' he yelled. 'Pull!'

Then it was there, sitting in the dust next to the deep hole. Lucillus took a long drink of the wine, still breathing hard, and looked back at the villa.

He didn't have the words to describe it. Just the size of it, easily twenty times larger than the roundhouse where his family lived, never mind the barns and stables that stood apart from the building. And the workmanship, each block of stone dressed and even. Part of him wanted to go and run his fingertips over them, to soak in the craftsmanship that was more than he could ever manage. Whoever lived here possessed the world.

A few more minutes and the lid was propped against the coffin, heavy leather straps under it all. Now there was nothing to do but wait. He leaned against the wagon. The sun beat down hard on the back of his neck and he wiped the flesh dry with a rag.

'All downhill on the way back,' Bellator said, studying the sky. 'If they hurry up we'll be home well before dark.' He sighed. 'Typical rich. They always take their time about things. Even death. Expect everyone else to wait on them.'

'Are there many like this?' Lucillus asked.

'Many what?' He coughed and spat.

'Houses.'

Bellator snorted.

'You ought to travel more. This is small compared to some. Go up near Eboracum, that's where the real money is. The proper Romans. You could fit four of these in one of the villas they build themselves around there. And more slaves than you can count.'

Then he stood straighter as the door opened.

Vassura had prepared herself carefully that morning. The maid had dressed her hair, sewing in the bun at the back, and she'd dressed in her best stola, the one he'd brought back six years before from a trip to Verulamium. She'd never worn it before, keeping it packed away in a chest, only pulling it out to hold against herself, to feel the quality of the material. Today, though, she knew nothing else would suffice.

What were they going to do? The question kept nagging at the back of her mind, the way it had since she'd seen all that remained of the man she'd loved. They needed *something* for the farm to survive, one of those miracles he said his Christian god could provide for the believers.

Morirex and Narina were waiting in the atrium, the maid

behind them. Vassura took a deep breath, picked up the sack and opened the door, moving with the gravity and weight of a widow.

She was beautiful, he thought. So clean, no dirt anywhere on her skin. The woman seemed to glow through her sorrow. She approached them with slow steps and greeted them all with a small bow of her head. The children stood just behind her, a boy with dark, curly hair holding hands with a girl who kept dabbing at her face.

'Thank you,' the woman said quietly. She bent, placing the sack inside the coffin and with a shock Lucillus realised that the story was true; there really was next to nothing of him left. The woman stood, then bent once more, opening her fingers to show a silver coin, letting it fall softly onto the sacking. 'For the ferryman,' she explained. 'Just in case.'

He watched her, taken by her sadness, the long, slim fingers with their golden rings. Minutes passed as she kept her gaze on the coffin, then she lifted her head and said, 'You can finish now.'

She stood, her arms protectively around the children's shoulders, as the men sweated and grunted, moving the coffin over the grave, then lowering it gradually out of sight. From the moment she realised that he was dead she'd known the place for this. He'd stood here so often, looking out over the valley as the sun rose. Sometimes she'd come out and stand by him, watching the way the light shifted and grew, and for brief moments she could understand why he cherished this place. Buried here, when his god called him he'd rise up and see all this one more time. Then, maybe, his shade would think of her again, with love.

The carter and the mason left, the sound of the wheels echoing loudly into the distance. The men began to fill in the grave, earth piling on the coffin until it was hidden. She remained in the same place, still there after the maid had taken the children indoors where it was cooler. She stood and kicked at a straggle of weeds, the only things that would prosper in this dry season.

What are we going to do?

Historical Note: Leeds might or might not have existed in Roman times. Although no real hard evidence has been found, a place called Cambodunum is briefly mentioned in writings, situated about 20 miles from Tadcaster on the road to Manchester. It's believed that the settlement was just south of the river, which was crossed by a stone ford. In 1901, as the grounds of Allerton Hall in Chapel

Allerton were being dug for development, a stone coffin was uncovered. There were only a couple of bones and a Roman coin inside.

Penda's Horse – 655

They brought him back in ignominy, his body slung over his horse, arms and legs hanging down. The man who'd been the king of Mercia didn't look so grand in death, just another empty bag of bones and flesh.

The mare, though, she was magnificent. Full fourteen hands high, with a white blaze like a star between her eyes, looking proud even after battle. When our king, Oswy, let the reins fall, I gathered them up and led her away.

'Boy!' Oswy yelled before I'd gone three paces.

'Yes Lord?' I was scared, he still had the blood lust in his eyes. Did he think I was stealing the beast?

'Throw the corpse off first.' He smiled. 'Then you can water the animal.'

With a grin I did as he ordered.

It was a grim day for battle. Late November and cold, with rain and sleet in the air. A time to dress warm and try to stay inside by the fire. But there was no chance for that. The scouts had ridden in early after a day of trailing Penda and the wild Welsh army with him.

They were close, should be here by noon. They looked tired and ragged, the scouts reported, after marching slowly south, on their way home with all the treasures they'd stolen and the weight of the souls they'd killed heavy on their hearts. Penda and his men were filled with the stain of sin, ones who'd refused to take Christ. Death was all they deserved. A long journey, exhausted. Murder in the name of God. And they were ripe for the plucking, or so my father claimed.

He was a thane, beholden to King Oswy of Northumbria. He'd come to fight when his master called and he'd brought me with him. I might have only been ten, too young to take part, but he believed I was ready to see war, to understand a campaign and battle.

'Remember, Leofric, you're here to watch and to learn,' he'd told me the night before as we made our beds close to the fire. 'And to help me if I need it,' he added with a smile. He made the sign of the cross. Northumbria was a Christian kingdom.

Oswy had ridden off with a handful of his men a few days before. Word came back that they'd harassed some of Penda's troops, attacking and then vanishing again before they could mount any defence.

'They're good tactics,' my father explained approvingly when he heard the news. He'd seen his share of battle and carried the scars to prove it. I was his oldest son. I was the one who'd wear the thane's mantle when he died. 'Each little raid kills two or three men. It's not many, but they mount up. More than that, it scares them. They'll keep looking over their shoulder. They'll be filled with fear, not knowing where we'll come from next. Or when.'

It was time to stop the pagan Penda. All the thanes were agreed on that. He'd killed Edwin, Oswy's father, long before I was born. He was a man with a hunger for power, a maw that was never satisfied, always gobbling up land. Not long ago he'd conquered Hwicce and put it under his rule. He'd killed and maimed and raped. Everyone knew he had the eagerness for more.

And this was the place we'd make our stand against him. Grimes Dyke, near the village they call Stanks, not far from the River Windwaed. Oswy had been cunning; he'd massed his force out of sight, hidden by the dyke that stood almost as high as three men. There was a wide ditch at the bottom and the beck running through it. How any man could get past that, I didn't know. I didn't see how we could be beaten.

'Don't go saying that,' my father warned grimly as he looked out to the land beyond. No enemy in sight yet. 'Penda has the luck of the devil.' He tousled my hair and smiled. 'But we have God, and we know who's stronger, don't we, boy?'

By the time the scouts arrived, we'd been up for hours. The women who travelled alongside had cooked for us, and now everyone sat, tense from all waiting. Tempers were on edge. They were ready to fight today. They wanted blood.

I wandered from group to group, listening to the gossip and the idle boasts that fill every camp. But I kept my distance from Oswy's guards, the ones who were sworn to protect him with their lives. They carried the glint of death in their manner, as if they'd as soon kill you as look at you.

There was a priest with us. He'd held his service that morning, giving his blessings and assuring us that God was on our side. I spotted him myself, on his knees in prayer. But he, too, carried a long sword.

The dyke had one weak spot, a place used as a ford across the beck. We'd spent the last two days building it up. Like everyone else, all the women and children as well as the men, I'd put in my hours digging and moving the earth until my palms and my fingers were covered in blisters. But I never complained.

The shout rose when they came into view, and suddenly everyone was scrambling. The time they'd all been waiting for had arrived, and still it seemed like a surprise.

I stood at the top of the dyke, staring into the distance. Penda was at the head of his force, a banner flying behind him, its colours caught by the breeze. He was surrounded by men on horseback, with far more on foot behind. It's wasn't hard to see that they outnumbered us. But if this was our day to die, then that was God's will.

Our men had been drilled. Each had his place, spears and their swords to hand. And every one of them had the order to wait. I could see it on their faces, though. Too many were eager for battle.

Penda and his troops came at a rush. The horsemen were in front, the gallop of their hooves on the ground like the rhythm of the dead. Those on foot followed quickly, running and yelling. Oswy had pricked them enough to make them reckless. They wanted revenge for the comrades they'd lost in the last few days.

'Stay back!' my father ordered, pushing me away towards the women before he took up his position. As soon as he left, I moved again. This was too important, too exciting. It was a sight I had to see. And I had my sling, I had some rocks in my pouch. I could play my part. We'd win, I felt certain.

The ditch halted them. Those in front dashed into it and found themselves trapped. The dyke was too high to climb. As men bunched up behind them, the cavalry in front couldn't turn and move back.

They were easy prey to the spears that rained down. Many of them fell swiftly and the others panicked, unable to fight properly. Finally the cavalry cleared enough space, trampling their own men as they tried to retreat. We'd damaged them. Their wounded screamed and howled like babies. I'd loosed rocks, one after the other, and seen some of their men fall. It was a child's weapon but it was effective.

I thought they'd give up. I didn't see how they could charge again, but after a few minutes, long enough to catch their breath, they returned, running and riding over their own casualties as they hurtled towards us. They never had a chance. The second wave fell as quickly as the first. They were men who'd stopped thinking, who only saw death.

And this time, when they retreated, Oswy gave the order to pursue them. It was something to see, our horsemen easing their mounts down the slope, then going full gallop in pursuit. I could pick out my father and the flash of his sword. Then our foot troops were among them, too.

Penda's men were exhausted. Two assaults had come to nothing, they'd been marching since dawn. They knew they were beaten. The field was a killing ground, nothing more than that. Our lord's men might as well have been slaughtering beasts.

Perhaps it lasted an hour. Maybe less. It roared in my ears and I couldn't look away. There was terror out there, but there was glory, too. I stood and I watched and I envied them.

From the moment our men charged it was obvious that we'd won. Penda and his men had no hope. The women and I set to hacking down the part of the dyke we'd built up just a day before. A way back for the victors.

I kept glancing over my shoulder for some glimpse of my father. Finally I could make out the shape of his horse, with its ears pricked high, prancing as it returned to camp.

My father had one hand grasping his arm as he rode, but he was smiling. And then came Oswy at the head of his picked men, leading Penda dead and bundled over the saddle of his mare.

The women were already down in the ditch, some of them out on the battleground, swarming and cackling like carrion crows. If they found someone alive, they slit his throat with their little knives, then took anything of value he possessed. It was how it had always been; how it would always be, as far as I knew. We'd won, the spoils were ours.

Someone was tending my father's wound, but he'd already given me a sign that it was nothing serious.

And then I saw Penda's horse.

I watered her and fed her as she shied around, frightened by the noise and the smell of blood. I talked gently to her, leading her in small circles until she calmed. A beautiful animal, worthy of a king. Even on the long journey she'd been cared for, brushed sometime recently, and she carried a saddle and bridle of beautifully-worked leather.

Once she'd eaten her fill and she was settled, I hobbled her and tied the reins to a tree. I didn't need to search for my father. He was walking towards me, his arm in a sling, Oswy at his side, holding a leather mug of ale.

'This is your son?' Oswy said.

'Yes, Lord,' my father said proudly. 'Leorfric, my oldest

boy.'

'How many did you kill today, Leofric?' the king asked.

'Three, Lord.' Shyly I produced my slingshot.

'He's a lad with an eye for good horseflesh.' Oswy nudged my father and laughed. 'Couldn't wait to look after Penda's horse.' He turned to me. 'You like that animal, boy?'

'Yes, sir.' My voice was so quiet I was amazed he could hear me.

Perhaps it was the ale, perhaps it was the generous flush of victory. But he stood there, assessing me as if he could tell my worth.

'Then she's yours, boy. Take her home and look after her well. When I need your service, though, you'd better ride her to help me.'

Historical Note: We do know that the Christian king, Oswy of Northumberland defeated and killed the pagan Penda of Mercia in the battle of Windwaed on November 15th, 655. What no one knows with certainty is where it happened, although there are two streets in Whinmoor – Penda's Way and Penda's Walk – that might have their origins in history. Certainly, a battle by Grimes Dyke is possible, but it's all speculation. The most curious aspect of it all is that the streets remember the loser in the battle, rather than the winner.

Five Stone Crosses – 946

I'd expected a mean little place, like the other Saxon villages in the kingdom. But as we approached, with the horses whinnying at some smell or other, it took me by surprise.

It was neat, cleaner than I'd imagined. The people looked well-fed, eyeing us with quiet suspicion as we arrived. Five of us, myself and four warriors, frightening, intelligent men with piercing eyes and dark glances. They'd proved themselves in battle often enough. A good escort for a holy man.

The church was wood, rough-hewn but carefully built. Their God might not be ours, but they worshipped him well. And outside stood five tall stone crosses, heavily carved and decorated with ornaments, scrolls and figures. I could pick out Weyland the Smith in one, from the story they love to tell at night. On others, there were angels, men, who knew what.

I dismounted, looking around. A man approached me hesitantly, bowing his head a little.

'You're welcome here, my Lord,' he said. 'I'm Hereward. The thane here.'

'Gunderic.' I nodded at him. 'Where are they?'

'Not here yet. One of my men spotted them a few minutes ago, still two miles away. Would you like something to drink after your ride?'

A girl came with a jug of ale and mugs. Out here we were on the edge of the kingdom. Our land, the Norse land, ended at the river a few yards away and on the hills to the east. It was autumn weather, most of the leaves already fallen, the branches as barren as crows. A grey sky and always the promise of rain on this damned island.

'King Erik, is he well?' Hereward asked. Inside, I smiled. Erik's name was one to make any conquered Saxon nervous. The Bloodaxe, they called him. It was true that he'd used the weapon often enough, but not for a few years now. These were the days of ruling, of words and diplomacy. Instead of the longships, we made marriage with the locals. I had, and Erik, too. His wife was the daughter of a nobleman from Strathclyde.

'He's in good health. Still strong as an ox.' Keep them wary of the man I'd served for twenty years, in Denmark and now here. We'd started as raiders and now people fawned in front of us. We were starting out own dynasties in Jorvik, a kingdom that might include all of England one day.

But not yet. That was why I was in this village of Loidis, standing close to the river, waiting to conduct a favoured guest back to meet my master.

'This church of yours,' I said, walking towards it. 'What are these crosses for?' I'd been all over the area in the last few years, but I'd never seen anything quite like this.

'To commemorate men who've died, Lord,' Hereward answered. 'Their sons have had them carved as memorials.'

'But why here?' I wondered.

'There's a ford at the river.' He pointed to a shallow area of the water. 'Plenty of people cross here. Some stay.'

Not many, from the look of the place. Houses spread in a line away from the church. Clean enough, yes, but hardly busy. I doubted there could be more than two hundred people in the whole of Loidis. But it had the church, more than most of these places. And it had these strange crosses.

A man ran up and spoke to Hereward.

'Cadoe will be here in a minute. King Domnall's come with him.'

I straightened my back. Royalty to escort the holy man? I hadn't expected that. They treated him with honour, so we had to do the same. But I was an important man in this kingdom. Not a king, perhaps, but certainly a lord, with lands of my own.

Ten of them. Domnall, his housecarls, heavily armed and glancing around constantly. They eyed my warriors with suspicion. And on a small mare, a thin man, simply dressed, his wild hair going grey. Cadroe. The holy man.

At first he didn't seem so remarkable. Then he turned to gaze at me and I saw his eyes. There was something in them, some fire, some certainty and passion. I'd never seen a look like it before.

But I knew my graces. First a bow to greet the king.

'Your Majesty.' My voice was loud enough for everyone to hear. 'I'm Gunderic, sent by King Erik to make sure his guest reaches Jorvik safely. He welcomes you all to his kingdom.'

No answer, other than a short nod of acknowledgment. I turned to Cadroe.

'My master looks forward to meeting and talking with you, sir.'

'And I look forward to seeing my dear Æthelberta again.' His eyes twinkled.

'My Lord?'

'Not Lord, not Sir. I don't have a title and don't want one,' he said.

'You're related to the king's wife?' I'd never heard this.

'Distantly, but yes. I'm related to Domnall, too.' He tilted his head towards the king who was talking to the thane. 'And we're all God's children, too.' For a moment I thought he was teasing. But the smile on his lips wasn't mocking me.

'King Erik is expecting us in Jorvik,' I told him, looking up at the sky. We'd spent the night in Sherburn and set out early to meet Cadroe; we'd be expected before dusk.

'Of course,' he agreed. 'But first, please, I'd like to preach for the people here. They rarely see a priest.' He stared at me. 'For their souls.'

Who was I to disagree? Treat him with respect; those had been my orders. As long as he didn't take too long, we'd still have time.

A word with Hereward, the sharp ringing of the bell that seemed to fill the sky. Another few minutes and the villagers came. A rag-tag bunch, the children as filthy as boys and girls anywhere. The women scared, full of tales about the Northmen. The men all farmers, with rough hands and weatherbeaten skin.

Once they'd gathered, Cadroe stood in front of the crosses and began to speak swiftly in his Saxon tongue. I spoke it passingly well – I had a Saxon wife myself, and my children switched between Norse and Saxon as if they were one language – but it always seemed ugly and guttural to my ears.

Yet a strange thing happened. As Cadroe spoke, it seemed to take on a musicality, a beauty I'd never noticed before. His words came quickly, too fast for me to follow them all. I glanced at the man quickly, then again. Before, he'd seemed small, someone not to be noticed in a crowd. Now he seemed taller, broader, and it was as if there was a light around him. I closed my eyes then looked again. But it was still there.

He spoke for five minutes, standing in front of those carved memories to men. I could understand how people thought him holy. There was some quality about him, something greater than any of us there, bigger than flesh, deeper than blood.

Cadroe finished with the sign of the cross and the words, 'May God go with you and protect you.'

And then, as his mouth closed and he began to walk towards me, he became an ordinary man again, with his grey hair, the lines on his face and thin body.

I didn't understand it. I couldn't explain it. But I'd ask him on the journey. We had ample time in the saddle ahead of us.

In less than five minutes we were ready to leave. Before I could mount my horse, though, Domnall beckoned me over.

'My Lord?' I asked.

'You saw, didn't you?' I opened my mouth to lie, but he continued, 'I watched your face. He has the message of God on his tongue for all who'll hear. Please, make sure your king listens to him.'

'That's my Lord's choice,' I reminded him.

'Of course.' Domnall smiled easily. 'But give your Lord one message from me, please. Tell him that men prosper more in peace than in war.'

'I will, your Majesty.'

I climbed onto my horse and we began to ride away.

Historical Note: In the *Life of St. Cadroe*, he's remembered as crossing between the kingdom of Strathclyde (ruled by Domnall) and the Norse kingdom (ruled by Eric Bloodaxe) at Loidis – the Saxon name for Leeds. It was a village on the border, used for crossings, and that gave it stature, even if it was still very small. When Leeds Parish Church was being rebuilt in 1838 workmen discovered pieces from five stone crosses that were dated back to the ninth and 10th centuries. The fragments have been put together to make the Leeds Cross, which now stands in Leeds Minster.

These could have been preaching crosses, which predated churches. But those would generally have come from an earlier period. It's far more likely that they were memorials erected to commemorate important people. Why would that be in Leeds? We'll never really know, but it's an indication that the village had real value and importance, certainly to the wealthy individuals who commissioned the crosses.

The Harrying – 1069

They came in the night, the Norman bastards. The first we knew was the screams and the sound of burning. My man was up quickly, grabbing his hoe and dashing out into the dark. As he pushed the door open I could see flames lighting up the sky.

We'd heard the word from folk passing on the road. William, him as ruled us now, he said, was sick of rebellion, of the lords and them who defied him. He'd sent out men to destroy the North.

For weeks people had been coming through in their ragged, desperate ones and two, a family and sometimes more, clutching what little they could carry, just seeking safety somewhere. We fed them, gave a place to sleep in a byre or a hut and saw them move on the next morning, hoping for a home to live free from sword and fear. Precious little chance of that in this land. In the church we prayed to the Holy Virgin that they'd leave us alone. But even as we mouthed the words we knew they'd arrive sooner or later.

Headingley had been famous once. I'd listened to the old men when I was a girl; I knew what all the tales said. How famous warriors, good men and great, would come from miles to gather at the Shire Oak and make their laws. I never pay mind to stories these days. They're just words and words won't feed my bairn. I'd lost three in blood and screams and pain before this one was born and every day I beseeched God to let him grow to his manhood.

I picked my sweet William up from the scraps of cloth that swaddled him and held him close to my breast. Keep quiet, I whispered. For the love of Jesu, suckle and stay quiet. His mouth found the nipple and he closed his eyes again as I huddled in the corner, trying to stay hidden from the terror and yelling that filled the world beyond my walls.

Embers gave the only light, shadows that moved around the room. A steer lowed helplessly somewhere before its cry was cut short and a man began to laugh. I cowered, pushing myself hard against the wattle, head down, trying to soothe my William.

They'd kill who they wanted and put it all to the torch. That was what they did; we'd been told. What could we do against the power of armed men on horseback, with evil in their heart? Ten houses in the village. All we had were hoes and scythes and the hunger that clawed at our bellies. What match was that?

There were screams that wouldn't end. I put my hands over

my ears but they remained. Even in her agony I knew her voice. Matilda, beautiful Matilda, and men doing what they always did in war and drink and rage.

I could smell the burning. Straw, flesh, meat. The shouting was loud, careless and urgent together. Matilda's voice fell silent.

Someone kicked the door open and came in, holding a brand. There was nowhere to hide from the light. A tall man, with blood smeared on the leather of his jerkin, the lust of killing on his lips. He grunted and dragged me upright. I just tried to hold William close, to keep him safe as I was pulled outside.

The dead lay on the ground. Ten, fifteen, twenty and more of them. I picked out my man, eyes blankly staring up at nothing, a deep wound in his chest. Matilda, the clothes ripped all the way to her flesh. Her throat had been cut.

The soldier casually threw his torch into my house. The days had been dry and the straw caught quickly as the fire began to crackle and roar. I kept my arms tight around William. A man grabbed my hair and pulled hard. I wanted to cry, to do anything, to vanish into the darkness. To take my son and live.

Without a word he slapped me so that I staggered, and someone else tore William away from me. I reached out. I screamed. I shouted. I begged while they laughed. They held him close to taunt me. When I lunged to reach him, they drew back again.

Then one of them gave an order with his strange words I couldn't understand. The tears ran down my cheeks. They held my head forcing me to watch as one of them lovingly drew his knife across my William's neck. The blood bubbled on his skin as his yelling turned to nothing.

They let me go then. I fell to my knees, cradling my lovely boy. His blood was warm against my flesh.

The men turned and began to walk away, leaving me there. The only one still alive here. Their testament. Their warning. Their memory. A warrior passed me, spat, and tossed his broken sword on the ground before me. I wanted to die, I wanted it more than I'd ever desired anything.

Long after they'd gone, when the sound of hooves had vanished and all that remained were the burning houses, I rocked my baby. I sang him soft lullabies and let my tears fall on his cheeks.

Through the night I whispered and cooed to him, stroked his soft hair. I spoke and I mumbled until my throat was raw. I told him every hope and dream I had stored for him, all the love I felt and the joy he'd given me.

By dawn he was cold.

Smoke from the ruins and black timbers were all that was left of Headingley. And the bodies tossed on the dirt. My man, my sister, my father, my friends. My son. The only building untouched was the church.

Finally I stood, picked up the ruined weapon and begin to hack out my William's grave. The earth was soaked with blood, coming up in wet clods. I dug all through the morning, not stopping for water or rest.

I had blisters on my hands but I kept working until I was three feet deep in the ground. Too far for the wolves ever to dig him out again. Safe for the coming of the Lord. I lowered him down, his face so beautiful even in death, and started to scoop the soil on top of him.

I said a prayer for his soul. God would listen. He'd been no more than a babe with no sin to stain him.

In the church I took hold of the rope, pulling until the bell began to toll. I let it ring for the memories of all those who were out there.

Outside, back in the light, I picked up the sword. I touched my man's lips then held the fingers to my own. And I walked away.

Historical Note: Much of the North didn't roll over and accept the conquest by William the Conqueror (or William the Bastard as he was known to contemporaries). In very brutal fashion, he asserted his authority, laying waste so much of the land. It's impossible to guess at how many people were killed as his troops rampaged, but mile after mile was laid waste. Leeds one of the very few manors to escape, but those all around suffered. Even a quick glance at the Domesday Book, produced in 1086, tells the grim story. It was a ruthless way to put down any opposition. I've taken the image of a woman being left a broken sword to bury her baby from Martin Carthy's striking version of the ballad "Famous Flower Of Serving Men."

The Holy Men – 1152

Perhaps they should have treated the villagers better, the abbot reflected. Six years and things were no better than when they'd first gone there. Worse, he knew. His horse walked on slowly, keeping the quiet pace of the others as they followed the winding track down through the trees.

They were close to a river. He caught glimpses of it from time to time. Another few minutes and they should be out of the woods. He pulled his cloak tighter around himself, over the pale Cistercian habit. There should be a village hereabouts; that was what he'd been told. At least it should be a place where he could find some dinner. He'd been riding since sunup and his stomach kept reminding him he was ready to eat.

They broke from the forest to see a plain stretching down to the water. A village, yes, but a poor one, smoke rising from the huts. And in the distance some other buildings, ramshackle things that seemed separate. What on earth were they, Abbot Alexander wondered?

This was supposed to be the quick way to Pontefract, but he was lost. Find your way to Kirkstall, he'd been advised, then it's just a few miles to Leeds. Ford the river and it's three hours more to Pontefract. With the castle high on the hill the town was supposed to be visible for miles. Alexander scanned the horizon but saw nothing like that.

What he did spy was a good area of fertile land. In his mind he could imagine an abbey here. The weather was softer, gentler here than up in Barnoldswick. That place was as barren and harsh as an old woman. And a fresh start, with a new village, new people.

It was still far from places but not too distant. Like the mother abbey, Fountains, and Ripon.

'We'll stop here for a little while,' he said to Brother Robert, who was riding alongside him. 'Surely they'll have enough to feed four travellers.' At least he hoped they would; he'd have a chance to judge how rich this place might be.

The old man who came out to greet them had a canny look about him, a smile on his mouth and a knowing gleam in his eye. Was he that transparent, Alexander wondered? But he gave the blessing and dismounted, the other three following his lead.

'I'm William, Master.' The old man bobbed his head after the abbot introduced himself. 'You're welcome here.' He made a gesture and one of the women went to find ale. 'We don't have too much but you're welcome enough to eat with us.'

'Thank you, my son.' And he was grateful; the thought of pushing on to Pontefract with an empty belly didn't appeal. It would just be pottage, but it would last him, and a feast at the castle would fill him tonight.

It was still warm enough to sit outside and eat. No meat, but he hadn't expected any. Still, there was good grazing land here. Safe land, too, safer than Barnoldswick where the damned Scots came down from the north to raid most months of the year. In his early days there the villagers had defended them. But after Alexander pulled down the village church, suddenly they made themselves scarce whenever there was trouble.

'Tell me, my son,' he asked William once the meal was done. 'What are those buildings over there?' He pointed at the odd structures he'd seen, a quarter of a mile up the river.

'Seleth and his followers, Master,' the man said proudly. 'Another holy man, just like you.'

The abbot raised an eyebrow. Like him? He'd never heard of a monastic house around here. And there was no church.

'What do you mean? What order does he belong to?'

William stood, sprightly for his age.

'You'd better meet him, Master. You'll see what I mean.'

The man was digging, working the ground as eagerly as the other five around him. But as William approached he looked up and wiped his hands on the sides of his jerkin.

'Brother,' he said, 'a pleasure to see you.' He weighed up the abbot, and for a heartbeat Alexander saw himself through the man's eyes. Portly, dignified, a man of words, not labour. 'My Lord,' the man said. 'Welcome. I'm Seleth.'

He spoke with an unusual accent, his voice almost bouncing over the words. An incomer from somewhere, a stranger. But William greeted him as a friend.

He studied Seleth's face. Scrawny, a thin beard, the pinched cheeks of hunger. But it was his eyes that caught Alexander's attention. They held a fire, the kind he'd seen before. It belonged to two types of people: saints and madmen. And out in this place, Seleth hardly looked like a saint.

'William says you're a holy man,' the abbot began doubtfully. 'You belong to an order?'

'No, Master,' Seleth replied, as if the idea shocked him. 'I'm here because the Virgin herself told me to come.'

'You had a vision?' In spite of himself, Alexander was impressed.

'Indeed, Brother, I did.'

Seleth had lived somewhere far to the south, he explained. A freeman, no wife or children, working his land and paying his lord. He'd been sleeping one night when suddenly his hut had been filled with light, bright as a summer midday. And then he'd heard the voice. A woman, with the most beautiful, sweetest tone he'd known in his life.

'She said, 'Arise, Seleth, and go to the province of York, and seek diligently in the vale called Airedale for a certain place called Kirkstall, for there shalt thou make ready a future habitation for the brethren who serve my son.'' He stayed silent for a moment, as if the words still filled his soul.

'What did you do?' Alexander asked gently.

'I asked who she was, of course.' His eyes were bright and there was a wide smile on his lips. She said "I am Mary, and my son is Jesus of Nazareth, the Saviour of the world." How could I disobey, Brother? I left home the next morning. It was more than a month of walking the roads before I found my way here. Some shepherds guided me out from Leeds. I built a small hut' – he pointed vaguely to one of the tumbledown structures – 'and knew I had my mission.'

'How do you live?' the abbot asked him.

'Roots and berries when I began.' He shrugged. 'My Lady guided me. Christian men who were passing gave me alms. William and the villagers here helped me. Within a few months a few others joined me, the people you see.' He was serious, every word intent. 'We pray and we work, just as the Holy Virgin commanded.'

'May God bless you here,' Alexander told him. 'But who leads you?'

'No one.' The thought seemed to take Seleth by surprise. 'Surely, Brother, the only one who can lead is God, and we all bow before him.'

'Quite.' The abbot made the sign of the cross.

As Alexander and his men mounted for Pontefract, he leaned down from his saddle and in a low voice asked William:

'Whose land is this?'

'William of Poictou, Master. He owns all this manor.'

'Thank you, and God bless you for the food.' A short benediction and they were on their way.

Leeds was nothing, a tiny hamlet just a handful of miles away with the ford over the Aire. As they splashed through the water, Alexander asked Brother Robert:

'What did you think of Kirkstall?'

'A sweet place, my Lord,' the monk replied after a little thought. 'The air was fresh, water close by. Why?'

'No matter.' The abbot returned to his thoughts.

It *was* a sweet place. Certainly better than Barnoldswick. No Scots to harry the folk this far south, and the winters would be less harsh. There was plenty of fertile land to cultivate. No village church to raise his ire with its loud services.

He'd been wrong to tear down the church in the village. He admitted that to the Papal legate. But the villagers, their priests and their clerks had taken against the monks from the beginning. They insisted on noisy celebrations at every feast day to ruin the contemplation of the soul. Destruction of the church had been the only solution. And the Pope himself had found in favour of the abbey when the villagers took their case to him.

He'd done what he could to make amends. He'd moved the abbey and even built them a new church, grander than the ruined old place they'd had. But they wouldn't be satisfied. They complained at every turn: to the abbot and to Henry Lacy, who held the land and had given the abbey its grant.

Alexander needed somewhere better. Somewhere calm. Still isolated, yet not quite so far from everything. Contemplation in Christ was a good thing, but an abbot had a duty to the realm, too.

They stayed in Pontefract for two nights. On their way home, after they crossed the ford in Leeds once more, Alexander turned to the others.

'I've a mind to see Kirkstall again,' he said. 'I'd like to talk more to this Seleth. I fear his soul is in mortal danger.'

The villagers came crowding round as they rode up; they'd never expected the monks to return. But after a cup of ale, the abbot quickly made his excuses and strode across the grass to see Seleth and his men.

Hermits. That's what they were. He'd seen the type before, and most of the ones he'd met were quite mad. Holy, perhaps, or maybe deluded, with a vision from the devil instead of Our Lady. And if they were heretics, they desperately needed redemption. The church could offer them that.

The man was still digging, not much further on than he'd been a few days before, it seemed. He stopped as Alexander approached, hailing the man with a smile.

'Welcome, Brother. I hadn't looked to see your face again. God goes with you, I trust?'

'I felt I had to come back,' the abbot told him.

Seleth smiled broadly, looking around.

'So you feel the pull of the place, too?' he asked eagerly. 'The holiness here?'

'God is everywhere, my son,' Alexander answered quickly. 'But since I left I've been worrying and praying about your souls.'

'Our souls?' Seleth frowned. 'We're doing God's work here. We've come to praise him. How can that bring shame on our souls?'

'I know you mean well,' Alexander said kindly. 'But how many of you are there?'

'Six.'

'Six men.' He sighed and shook his head. 'So few. All of you, you're disciples without a master.'

'We're equal before the Lord,' Seleth said.

'In heaven, yes,' the abbot countered. 'But on earth it's a different order, my son. Here it's masters and men. That's what God ordained, and that is how we must live. After all, the disciples followed Jesus. But they weren't his equals, were they?'

'No,' Seleth admitted.

'And where's the priest to minister to you?' Alexander continued. 'A man needs to confess, to have his sins absolved.'

'There's a church in Leeds. We can go there.'

'My son,' Alexander began gently. 'I know your heart belongs to God. I can see it in your eyes. But religion and worship have rules. Do any of you speak Latin? Do you have your letters? Can you take the service?'

'No.'

'A holy order can give you that. Prayer. The beauty of work and contemplation. A chance to free your soul.' He looked around. 'This land here, it's beautiful, it could be something grand. Don't you see that?'

'If you say so,' Seleth agreed doubtfully. 'It does fine for us. It supplies our needs.'

'And it could be so much more, my son. That's what God desires. He put us on this earth to use the land, to glorify Him in our work, to produce abundance.' He paused for a moment. 'You say

Our Lady told you to come here.'

'She did.'

'Then perhaps God Himself guided my footsteps to this place, to show me what it might be like. It takes men to make something great. More than six men.'

'What do you propose, Brother?' Seleth asked suspiciously.

'To bring my monks from Barnoldswick to here. To found a new abbey at Kirkstall. A wondrous place to worship. For *all* of us. To His glory. '

'We're happy here as it is.'

'God wants us to have all the bounty of this place, my son, not just some small portion of it. With priests, with a master, your souls won't be in danger. You'll be able to live the life of the spirit you desire.'

They were fine words, Alexander knew that. He'd spent the last two days conjuring them up and spinning his argument. No doubt this Seleth was devout. But a place like this was wasted on him. He was a simple man, untutored, unlettered. A man like that born to follow, not to lead. A good fellow, certainly. And the church needed good fellows; they made excellent monks.

'I don't know, Brother.'

'Think on this: Perhaps your role in God's plan was to come here first, to prepare the ground and show it to me.' He opened his arms, as if illustrating what it might become. 'There can be grandeur here and you'll have played your part in this. Each of us has his part in God's plan.' His voice turned solemn. 'But remember, a man's soul is his only wealth. And without it, you can never reach heaven.'

He made the sign of the cross and laid a hand on Seleth's shoulder. The man looked beaten down, defeated.

'You've done good work here,' the abbot told him. 'The Lord will thank you for that. And you can still do good work as part of the abbey. You'll be an honoured man, I will promise you that.'

As the small party rode away, Alexander turned to Brother Robert.

'Tell the other two there's been a change of plan. We're going to stop and see Henry Lacy on our way home.'

The monk was startled.

'Why, my Lord? Is something wrong?'

'Not at all,' the abbot answered with a smile. 'I just want him to write to Walter Pictou. There's a way for Walter to cleanse his immortal soul.'

Historical Note: According to some sources, a man named Seleth, who lived in the south of England, did experience a vision, when the Virgin Mary told him to come to Kirkstall, to settle there and worship. And it's certainly true that the monks at Barnoldswick had a tempestuous relationship with the local villagers and moved from there to Kirkstall. One account has Abbot Alexander passing through Kirkstall on business and persuading Seleth to become part of the Cistercian order. But, of course, we'll never know the truth of the matter.

On Briggate – 1207

This month he was Maurice de Gant.

It was impossible to know how he'd style himself. Sometimes it was de Gant, his real name. Then he'd change it to Maurice Paynel, taking on his mother's maiden name. It was Paynel had signed the charter to create the borough of Leeds; now de Gant was the one who raged about not seeing any return from it yet.

He strode around the hall in the manor house, shouting and complaining.

'Where's the money?' he yelled. 'You said it would bring in money.'

The two advisers looked at each other. They knew the truth. Maurice Paynel, Lord of the Manor of Leeds, had insisted on creating the new town. He'd heard of others doing it successfully and believed he could, too.

He was the one who pushed and prodded. They'd told him it was doubtful, that it might be years before he saw any income from it. But Paynel – de Gant – was young and headstrong. He believed he knew better.

And he was desperate. He'd inherited a manor that was mortgaged to Aaron the Jew in Lincoln, and had been for well over a decade. De Gant had land, he had a title, but he had no money apart from the sums the moneylenders would grant him. His debts were growing year on year.

'Where are the tradesmen?' de Gant asked de Harville the adviser. The man pulled his robe closer around his shoulders, as if he was chilled.

'We told you, my Lord. These things take time. We have ten tenants, each of them paying 16 pence in rent.'

'Ten!' He picked up a wine goblet and threw it towards the wall. But it fell short, landing in the rushes and spilling the drink onto the ground. 'What's the use in ten? I need the place full.'

His idea was ambitious. Sixty plots, thirty on each side, making sure the street was wide enough to hold a market. A place for craftsmen, townsmen who'd make their living from their skill or trade. They could sub-divide their plots, even sell some of their holdings. It was generous, especially when each plot also had half an acre of land away from the new town to grow food. The men who moved there would owe no service, only rent.

But the advisers were doubtful. Paynel – he was Paynel

whenever he talked about his new charter – was full of enthusiasm, but the other men were older. They understood the reality.

'It won't happen in a month,' de Harville told him. He was a dour man, used to life's setbacks, gaunt, spare in his frame and with his money.

'He's right, Lord,' agreed le Seul, the other adviser. He was rounder, with full red cheeks, most of the hair gone from his head. He'd known de Gant's father, Robert, as unlucky a man as had ever owned land. A fool, and soon parted from his money through this scheme or that. It looked as though his son would be as bad. 'You need the right people. Those who'll stay. It takes time to find them.'

'God's balls, you've got no adventure.' Paynel's eyes were blazing with excitement. He knew it couldn't fail. And now, half a year on, he was berating them.

'What are you doing to bring tenants?' de Gant roared.

'We've put word out in York and Pontefract,' de Harville replied cautiously.

'As far away as Derby and Lincoln,' le Seul added.

'Then where are they?' Maurice tore the purse from his belt and tossed it on the table. No jangle of coins, just a quiet slap of leather. 'They're not bringing me any money. Get people in here.' He stormed out of the room, disappearing up the wooden staircase to the solar.

De Harville and le Seul walked the length of the street, from the edge of the open fields at the north all the way down to the river. Most of the plots were still marked off with ropes. Some had houses that had been erected quickly, little more than huts.

'He's like a child throwing a tantrum,' le Seul said. 'But he's always been that way. His mother indulged him when she should have beaten him.'

'We won't be able to please him.'

'We told him the truth. God's blood, we told him often enough before he signed the charter. But he had it in his mind and he didn't want to listen.'

'They think they can trick me,' de Gant complained to his wife. She was sewing by the light of a candle, working some new linen for him. 'Anything to avoid responsibility.'

'What are they saying, Maurice?' Catherine was a woman with a quick mind and a good memory. She knew her husband's good points but she was also keenly aware of his faults.

'That I was the one who wanted this new town.'

She stabbed her needle into the fabric and looked at him.

'But that's true,' she said coolly. She was the only one who could talk to him this way, the only one who dare give him some truths. 'They advised you against it because it wouldn't bring in any quick revenues.'

'We've had ten tenants in six months,' he said in his defence.

'Ten tenants, sixty plots.' She gave an expressive shrug. 'This won't be our answer, my love. Not for a few years, anyway.'

'Then what are we going to do?' de Gant asked. 'Tell me that.'

Catherine smiled.

'I have an idea.'

De Harville and Le Seul stood by the river, where the new street vanished into a ford and continued in a road on the other side. There was a sharp wind here, enough to make them both shiver in the October cold.

'I have a thought,' Le Seul said finally. 'If there was a bridge here it would attract more people. Leeds would be easy to reach. That might bring more tenants. And he could charge a toll.'

'He won't go for it.' De Harville dismissed the idea. 'Where would he find the money to build it? You know how he is. Unless he believes the idea is his, he won't back it.'

'There'll be one, sooner or later.' He turned his head to look back up the street. 'Once all those are filled and there's a market every week, we'll need one.'

De Harville smiled.

'That may not be in our lifetime, my friend. Come on, we'll freeze out here.'

Historical Note: Maurice Paynel (aka Maurice de Gant) signed the charter for the building of a new borough in 1207. He needed money – his father had mortgaged the manor of Leeds in 1191. It was an opportunity to merchants and craftsmen, but it wasn't an immediate success. The long street (from the Headrow down to the Aire) became known as Briggate (which means Bridge Street), although the first mention of a bridge over the river comes a century later. But perhaps it was built before then…

The Murder – 1318

Sunday, with only the prospect of piety until bed. Robert de Ledes was bored and it wasn't yet eight in the morning. He'd washed and broken his fast, just waiting until it was time to leave for service at St. Peter's. A purse dangled by its strings from his belt. He reached into it and toyed with the pair of dice.

What use was a bloody Sunday? He could have been hunting or gambling instead of listening to the priest and bowing his head with the others in Leeds. So many of them stank, their clothes as filthy as the hovels where they lived.

With a sigh Robert strapped on his sword. It was a good weapon, a gift from his father, with silver on the pommel and brass worked into the scabbard. A rich man's weapon, and why not? His family had money, more than most in the ville. North Hall stood near the top of Briggate, built just twenty years earlier, before the bad weather had started turning the crops foul, summer after summer.

Some starved, but his father made sure the family wasn't among them. Money meant power, and his father used it well.

Down by Kirkgate he spotted William de Wayte. An idiot who believed himself a thinker. Ungainly, with no charm beyond his ability to lose at dice. More money than brains. He was with his page and John de Manston, a cousin visiting from somewhere – William had told him, but he'd forgotten.

'Well met,' Robert cried, and soon the pair of them were throwing the dice against the wall of a house while de Manston and the page strolled on to the church. The bell was just beginning to peal for service when Robert give a final flick of his wrist. A six and a one.

'Seven,' he told William. 'I win.' He began to rise, scooping up the dice and putting them into his purse. 'You can settle with me later.'

'I won't pay a cheat. I didn't see what came up on that last throw.'

'Be careful with that tongue,' Robert warned. 'You saw it as well as I did: six and one. Or are you calling me a liar?'

'I'm calling you a cheat.'

Without even thinking, Robert drew his dagger, blade glinting in the summer light, and advanced on William.

'Do you think you're man enough?' he asked with relish.

He knew William; they'd grown up together. Brave enough with some friends behind him, a coward on his own.

'Enough!'

Robert turned and saw the reeve coming towards him, a look like fury on his face. His assistant came behind, a burly man with a rough face, the miller alongside, always ready for a scrap. Robert lowered the dagger.

'No fighting on the Sabbath,' the reeve ordered. Robert nodded. Eyes turned to William, who agreed reluctantly. 'Now get to church and say your penance.'

He snored through the service, the Latin that no one but the priest understood. The summer's day was warm, the smell from the bodies around him rank. Robert only stirred for the final blessing, staying to talk to the priest and explain why his father hadn't attended. He'd needed to see to his manor out by Harrogate, remaining there a few days.

Finished, he strolled out into the sun, blinking and squinting. The door banged shut behind him and he heard the sexton lower the bar. The man couldn't wait to see him gone and be done with his duties.

He'd only taken one step when he saw them. William, de Manston, and the page, the three of them coming closer with their weapons drawn. Robert rested his hand on the hilt of his sword.

'Does it take three of you to argue with me?

'I won't be called a liar by you,' William said.

Robert's face curled into a smile.

'What would you have me call you, then? Blind? A coward?'

The fight was quick. No more than a few seconds. Three on one was no battle. But Robert had trained with the sword. His fencing master had fought with the king and had taught him to spot an opening and strike at his enemy's weakness.

It was over as soon as William fell to the ground, hands trying to staunch the blood spurting from his stomach.

He'd never killed a man before, but he knew, he *knew*, as he saw the life leave William's eyes.

'Christ's blood,' De Manston said slowly, raising his eyes to look into Robert's face. 'That's murder.' And with a yell he came on.

The air in the Marshalsea prison was foul. The vapours of the dying and the damned everywhere. At least his father's money bought

Robert a cell to himself and food from the cookshops outside the walls.

He'd wanted to see London, but not this way. On trial for his life, for the murder of William de Wayte. A matter too grave for the manor court, a capital crime that could only be judged in the capital.

And he'd been here for three months now. He lived from his father's purse, money to pay the toothless jailer who kept him here. He ate roast beef, roast chicken; the straw and the rushes in his cell were changed each month.

He had visits from his lawyer, an oily, nervous man from the Inns of Court who assured him the case was progressing quickly. Another month, or two or three, and it would be heard. But no certainty about the verdict.

However he lived here, nothing could block out the screams and shouts from the prison. Those who had little, begging for something. Some relief, some end. He'd seen them taken out to be hanged, men and women with their heads bowed. Some walking, others dragged to the gallows as hundreds cheered at the spectacle.

He'd been brought here in chains that rubbed his flesh raw as he rode the King's highway. Still had the scars on his legs and his face from when de Manston and the page fell on him outside St. Peter's. They'd beaten him bloody, the chaplain joining them. Beaten him until he passed out and then beaten him more before they rolled him into the ditch that separated the church from the graveyard. Then they walked away and left him for dead. If one of the North Hall servants hadn't found him he'd have been a corpse.

As it was, he was eight weeks recovering. For three days his mother prayed over him. A physician came with his unguents and potions. And eventually he came back to life, with all the marks of what he'd endured. Then William's father had him arrested for murder. A criminal. A killer.

Robert had given his testimony at the manor court, how he was attacked first. Now he'd have to give it again, and his life depended on that and the witnesses his father could gather.

The London jury listened all day, first to Robert, how he'd just defended himself when he was attacked, then to the witnesses de Wayte produced. De Manston, the page, the chaplain, others who claimed to have seen things that Robert knew had never occurred. Then those for his defence. And over each testimony was the spectre of the hangman. And finally it was done, the last oath sworn, his life in the hands of the grim-faced men who shifted on their seats.

'Robert de Ledes, the jury finds you innocent in the murder of William de Wayte. You can go from this court a free man.'

Cheers, shouts of outrage, but he barely noticed them. It was done.

Historical Note: The killing of William de Wayte by Robert de Ledes is the first recorded murder in Leeds, but in all likelihood there'd been a number that had happened in the years before. It did occur at the Parish Church of St. Peter, and de Ledes was beaten and left for dead after. On his recovery, charged with murder, he was taken to London to be tried. In an age where more depended on how believable and credible the witnesses seemed, he found some who carried more weight. He was found innocent of murder.

Mr. Rockley's Pride – 1490

Never was there a place in Leeds like Rockley Hall. Never a place so grand in the North of England – it could have stood with the best dwellings of the capital. Certainly, we'd seen nothing like it before in its elegance and its beauty. But Leeds had never seen a man like Henry Rockley before, either. And I should know, because I had the honour to serve him.

To call him the bailiff of the manor of Leeds does him no real justice. It was a title far below his true rank. He leased the King's Oven in the manor, where every family baked their bread by law, and that brought in a tidy penny. He leased land that others rented from him for their fields and their houses. He was the man who collected the tax on all the cloth sold in Leeds. He was in every way a gentleman and I was proud to be part of his household.

A pious soul, too. Each Sunday all of us in the house would process to the Parish Church to pray. People understood that Henry Rockley was a man of substance.

He even designed this house himself. It had come to him in a dream, he claimed, and I for one believe it. For he was a man of vision, one who saw what needed to be done then went and worked until the task was complete.

Rockley Hall lay at the top of the city, on the Lower Head Row, its windows to the front gazing out to the country, to the fields and meadows the master leased. From the back it looked down over the town towards the church. I bade the servants clean the windows each Saturday, rain or shine, so Mr. Rockley could see all he loved so dear.

He paid me well to run the house. Six pennies a day and all found, a fortune to a man like me, low-born but with hope. I had my own room by the stairs to the undercroft, with a hearth to keep me warm in winter. The rest of the servants had their quarters in the eaves, men in one wing, women in the other, and no heat for the cold nights.

The hall was timber and limewash, with a neat slate roof and two wings shaped to form a U. The entrance lay at one end of the central section. At first look it jarred the symmetry with its position. But I came to understood it was a perfect place for a wagon or carriage to turn around. The master had thought of everything

Mr. Rockley loved that house. There was all of himself in it. He'd have built it all himself if only he'd had the time and the skill.

As it was, he supervised every part of the construction, making sure it conformed precisely to his plans. Because builders, as everyone knows, are sly men. They'd shave corners here and here to increase their proat each turn. But Henry Rockley was too wily to allow that.

He worked long hours, but when he returned in the evening it was to a place that brought him joy. I'd wait on him, whether food or wine, and he'd smile as he sat in the hall, taking in the heat of the large fire.

'Martin,' he'd tell me with a sigh of contentment, 'this is what makes life worthwhile.'

His wife and children would be waiting upstairs, eager to see him. But he'd linger, spending time with the house as a man might with a mistress. Small, stolen hours of pleasure.

'When I'm old,' he said as I poured his third glass of wine one night, 'I shall give up business and spend all my time here.'

I didn't believe it. He was a man who didn't feel alive unless most of his waking hours filled with one demand of work or another.

And so it continued until the autumn of the year 1490. It was just good fortune that I was working in the hall, bringing the accounts for the house up to date. I heard something at the door. Not a knock, more a scratch. A mystery. At first I ignored it, but when it came again, then once more, I went to see what the sound might be.

It was the master, with barely enough strength to stand. At first I thought he must have been attacked and sent the groom running off for the physician while I helped Mr. Rockley inside, his weight heavy against me. He was so pale, so weak, that I believed death might claim him.

After I settled him in the bed and gave him a drink of ale, I paced and fretted until the doctor had examined him.

'Keep him quiet,' he ordered. 'No excitement. Make sure he rests as much as he can. I've seen this before in gentlemen who labour too hard. His humours are deeply out of balance.'

'Will he die?' I asked. I was frightened; it was the question that had been gnawing at me since I saw him.

'He may,' the physician said, his voice suddenly very sober. 'That's in God's hands.'

For two days the Lord weighed him. The master's wife and children came to pray by his bedside, making their peace. I tended him, sleeping on the floor of his chamber when I could take some rest.

And then came the miracle. He opened his eyes, look at me

and asked:

'What day is this, Martin?'

'Thursday, Master,' I replied in amazement.

'Of course,' he said and fell asleep once more.

He didn't wake again until the next morning. By then the colour had returned to his flesh and he breathed more easily. I summoned the physician and after an examination, he declared:

'God has been gracious.'

It might have been God that spared him, but that didn't stop the man taking his fee as he left.

Mr. Rockley was weak, of course. It was two more days before he could stand comfortably, another week before he was able to leave the house. Even then he leaned on my arm as we walked slowly down to the church.

He wanted to give thanks and stayed for an hour, praying on his knees in front of the altar. As I helped him up, he was smiling, his face full of joy.

'A chapel,' he told me. 'A chapel for the glory of God.'

And he built it. He was a man of deeds, not empty words. He talked with the priests and offered his money to endow the Rockley Chapel. The Rockley Quire, as people called it. It was full of grandeur, with a silver cup for the holy wine and plate for the wafers, a jewelled cross and some of the most beautiful tapestries he could order, gold thread as part of the weave.

The master visited the church each day, choosing me to accompany him as he gave thanks for his life. His talk started to move from profit and loss and the business of his account books to things more eternal. The qualities of the soul, of goodness and evil, and how a man might find its way to Heaven.

He changed. The master became more thoughtful. A man of charity, giving alms to the beggars he passed on Briggate. He'd always been a good man, of course, but now he seemed to shine. Whatever had happened when he came close to death, the alteration remained. There was a radiance around him, it seemed to me.

Mr Rockley gloried in God. He still attended to his business, of course, but he gave away much of his money, instead of being filled with the desire to acquire more. He lost the sin of pride in all things but one.

Rockley Hall.

That remained his joy.

He lavished care on it. Fresh limewash every year, an

extravagance far beyond most men. The wood – wainscoting, floors, banisters, furniture – was polished every week. Sometimes he'd come home from a trip to York with a Turkey rug he'd bought, thinking it fine to sit here or there, like a man might return with a present for a mistress. Or he'd have a piece of well-worked pewter to display with the plate.

He loved his family, make no mistake about that. He doted on his wife and his children. But it always seemed that the house had the deepest place in his heart.

Once he'd fully recovered, Mr. Rockley summoned the lawyer and changed his will. He left money for mass to be said each day for his soul and for the upkeep of the Rockley Quire. And he ordered bequests for all his servants, including myself. The most generous of masters.

And, as long as he lived, he made sure there was never a place in Leeds like Rockley Hall. No rival for splendour or grace. No place with more beauty and care lavished upon its four walls.

Historical Note: Rockley Hall stood for many years at the bottom of the Headrow (where Rockley Hall Yard is today). It was still there at the end of the 17th century, as Ralph Thoresby described it. After Rockley's death in 1502 the building passed through several hands and had many uses. When it was finally torn down, the good oak timber formed the joists of the building that replaced it. On a personal note, the Yard was where some ancestors of mine had the premises for their painting and decorating business in the 1850s.

The Cloth Searcher – 1590

'Hoping is not enough, sir!' Randall Tenche berated the younger man. 'You have to act with certainty. Certainty!'

Ebenezer Lister was sweating inside his doublet. It wasn't just the warm July weather. He'd been nervous about reporting his doubts to Tenche, knowing how excitable and precise the man could be.

It wasn't as if he wanted the duty of Cloth Searcher. And by rights he shouldn't have had it. But with Tenche so often gone from Leeds these days, it had to fall on someone. The merchants had elected him as Tenche's deputy in the post of Cloth Searcher. So, each Tuesday and Saturday morning that Tenche was away, Lister was on Leeds Bridge, examining the lengths of woven cloth displayed for sale on the parapets.

The office brought great responsibility. If Leeds was ever going to be a force in the wool market, the merchants argued, if it was ever going to be greater than York or Beverley, then the quality of the cloth had to be the highest. Unassailable. And so the Cloth Searcher inspected each piece to make sure it met the standards – and they were demanding. Any not deemed adequate were rejected.

Yesterday Lister has passed a piece that might not have been good enough. He had his doubts but he'd let it go because he wasn't sure. Tenche hadn't been here – he'd been on the road, coming back from Wollaton in Nottinghamshire. Now Lister had confessed his fault and he was feeling the sharp edge of Tenche's tongue.

He stood and took it, knowing he'd done the wrong thing.

'God in heaven, man. Don't you want Leeds to have the best reputation in England?'

'Of course.' Lister swallowed.

'Who bought the piece?'

'Mr. Atkinson.'

'I'll go and see him later. If it's not good enough, perhaps we can recompense him and it can just vanish. Who was the clothier?'

'Thompson. From Whitkirk.'

'I know him,' Tenche said with a nod. 'He's always been a sly devil. I've had to refuse his work before.' He sighed. 'Never mind, never mind. Just be more careful next time.'

'Will you be here for Saturday's market, sir?'

Tenche fixed him with a stare.

'I think I'd better make sure I am, don't you?'

Alone, Randall Tenche paced around the room. His strongbox sat in one corner. He knew to the last farthing what lay inside. Always be certain of what you have; that was what his father had drummed into him, and he lived by it. The knowledge let him know what risks he could afford to take.

Bidding on the tapestry work the year before had been the biggest chance yet. So far it had paid off handsomely. £50 per annum from Sir Francis Willoughby at Wollaton Hall to execute on cloth the designs a painter created. Handsome money.

He'd been able to pursue the opportunity after two Flemish refugees came to Leeds and asked him for work. All he'd had to offer them was weaving, and they did a good job at it, both of them employing their families to help. But their experience was tapestry work; Flanders was renowned for that.

He stored the fact at the back of his mind. When he heard that Sir Francis was seeking tapestry makers he'd written the man a letter, explaining that he had the workers and imploring Sir Francis to enquire about his reputation. There was no man more honest than Randall Tenche. Everyone in Leeds said so.

After some negotiations he'd signed the contract. A huge sum for himself and six shillings and eight pence to each of the workers for every tapestry. His workers would create them in wool and silk, however Sir Francis demanded. They did everything from dyeing and spinning to weaving. And they'd done it all very well; Sir Francis was pleased with the result, displaying them in the rooms at Wollaton Hall.

But on this last trip Sir Francis had a new request: along with the silk, Willoughby wanted the tapestry picked out in gold. It was in the contract, Tenche knew that, but this was the first time the man had invoked it.

'I want something grand,' Sir Francis told him. 'Something fit…for a queen.' And he'd let the words slowly settle.

So that was it. He was expecting Her Majesty to visit Wollaton Hall and he wanted a gift for her. He'd brought back the sketch, a woodland scene with nymphs and deer. Crudely drawn, but the weavers could make art out of it.

The door opened and Catherine, the servant, entered.

'Mrs Tenche wants me to tell you it's time for dinner, sir.'

'Very well. I'll be along shortly.'

She left and he sat at his desk for a moment. Where in the name of God was he going to find gold thread in Leeds?

'You've been restive since you came back yesterday,' Meg observed as he pushed the food around the pewter plate. 'Don't waste it. That's good beef. I selected it at the Shambles myself.'

She was a prim woman, always cautious of luxury, even though they could well afford a good life. Meg always dressed plainly, as if all the extravagant silk in a gown could bring sin and danger on her. Every Sunday she attended the Parish Church faithfully. Not simply the morning service that he snored through, but all three during the day, dragging their children along with her.

His son Nicholas was wolfing down his food. Fourteen now, he'd be leaving for the Lowlands in another month. Tenche had arranged the boy's apprenticeship with a merchant there. Let him learn that end of the business. He'd already been working in Leeds for three years, since he left the Grammar School, and he knew it as well as anyone. By the time he was ready to take over from his father he'd have a thorough understanding of how everything worked. And he'd have contacts. Contacts, they were the invaluable thing about business. Not what you knew but *who* you knew. Nicholas would do well. His head was firmly on his shoulders.

His daughter, Hannah, though, she was a different matter. She seemed to have no interest in anything. When pressed by her mother, she'd embroider a little, putting the needle aside as soon as she could. She was a year younger than her brother, pretty enough, Tenche supposed. He wondered if he might find a suitable husband for her soon. At least she wouldn't be brooding around his house then.

'The meal's fine.' He took a bite, chewing slowly to illustrate his enjoyment, and followed it with a gulp of wine. 'I need to go,' he said as he stood from the table. 'I have an appointment.'

Dieter and Josef were brothers. They'd made their way to Leeds from Flanders together, wives and children travelling with them. They shared an old house near the top of Vicar Lane, looms set up on the ground floor, everyone living higgledy-piggledy upstairs. It seemed an odd arrangement to Tenche, but they were content enough with it.

He gave them the drawing, listening as they made their suggestions and pointed out what might work and what wouldn't. Finally he said:

'This is meant as a gift for Queen Elizabeth,' and that left them quiet. 'It needs to be the best you've ever made.'

'It will be,' Josef assured him. Over the last three years his voice had taken on the Leeds vowels to mix with his guttural speech. It wasn't attractive. 'The best ever.'

'There's one more thing,' Tenche told them. 'Sir Francis wants gold thread worked in to this.'

'That won't be easy,' Josef said after some thought. 'We've worked in gold before, a long time ago. It's very delicate. Very expensive, too.'

'Sir Francis understands that. He's paying us a little extra.'

'Good, good.' Josef nodded approvingly.

'Where will we find the thread?' Dieter asked, sitting on the bench with his mug of ale. He drank all through the day but he was always in control of himself, hands steady and mind alert. He was the quieter brother, rarely speaking. 'I've never seen any gold thread here.'

'Nor have I,' Tenche admitted. 'I hoped you might know.'

'York,' Dieter told him. 'Isn't that where your archbishop lives? All those rich garments, they must have it for sale there.'

Tenche smiled.

'Of course. I'll go there tomorrow.'

He felt relieved. One problem solved.

'Buy the best quality,' Josef advised. 'If you don't, it will just snap.'

'I will.' It was for the Queen. He wasn't going to cut corners there.

Atkinson was in his warehouse behind the big house on Briggate. As long as there was daylight, that was where he spent his time. Often long past that, too, his servant almost having to drag him in to supper with his family.

He was a man of profit. Atkinson lived for the excellent bargain and the well-struck deal that brought him good money. He revelled in it. In his forties, hair gone grey, he walked with a small stoop, his face always serious, his gaze forever searching around.

'Tenche,' he said. It was his normal greeting, terse and non-committal. 'How was Nottinghamshire?'

'Fine.' He wasn't about to say much. Keep your mouth closed, his father had also said, and it had proved to be powerful advice over the years.

'We missed you at the market yesterday.'

'I heard you bought some cloth.'

'Bought and already sold. A fair price for it, too.' Atkinson gave a satisfied smile. 'Shipping it out in the morning.'

'There might be a problem, sir. Mr Lister came to see me this morning. He has his doubts about the quality of the cloth you purchased.'

'Doubts?' The word seemed to confuse him. 'What kind of doubts? He passed it. He never said a word to me.'

'He thinks he might have acted rashly, that it might not be good enough.'

'Too late now.' Atkinson waved the idea away. 'It's bought and paid for.'

'I'd still like to look at it, if you'd be so good…'

'No,' the man said firmly. 'I spent half the morning packing it. I'm not going to get it out again just because young Lister can't make up his mind. If he doesn't know how to be a Cloth Searcher, maybe we need someone else.' He stared at Tenche. 'Or one who's always here for the markets.'

'You know the reason I was away,' Tenche said.

'You've been gone a great deal in the last year.' Atkinson seemed to warm to his idea. 'It's not good enough.'

'It's business, Hezekiah.' He tried to make his tone friendly.

'No doubt it is,' Atkinson said with a quick nod. 'But there's business here, too, and that's a damned sight more important to me.'

'Let me at least take a look at the cloth. The reputation of Leeds stands on everything we send out.'

'Your fellow passed it, didn't he?'

'Yes,' Tenche agreed cautiously. 'But –'

'No buts.' Atkinson slammed his fist down on the desk. The noise rattled through the warehouse. 'He passed it. If he's having second thoughts now, it's too late. Do I make myself clear?'

'Absolutely, Hezekiah.' He spoke through gritted teeth. 'But remember: the trade here is still young. We've worked hard to gain a reputation. All of us. It wouldn't take much for it to vanish.'

'Then perhaps the Cloth Searcher should do his job thoroughly and not rely so much on someone who's little more than a boy.' Atkinson glowered at him. 'That cloth leaves tomorrow, and damn the man who tries to stop it.'

Tenche turned away, bidding the man good day. He could argue until his face was blue but he'd have no joy here. Atkinson was determined and Tenche had no power to stop things. The man was right; if Lister had passed the cloth, there was nothing more to be done, and Atkinson had never been a man to care about right or wrong, not when he weighed it against profit.

He knew that for the next fortnight he'd spend every night tossing and turning each night, hoping the quality of the cloth was good enough and that the buyers were satisfied. Only then would he be able to sleep properly. Ultimately the responsibility was his. He'd taken on the job of Cloth Searcher. It had been an honour, one he'd sought, and he'd neglected it.

No more. He'd make sure he was at the cloth markets. Each Tuesday and Saturday on the bridge, Lister with him until he was certain he could trust the lad.

Historical Note: Randall Tenche truly was deemed an honest man by everyone. His contract with Sir Francis Willoughby was very lucrative – £50 was a huge sum in Elizabethan times – and he made sure everything was executed well. He was also the Cloth Searcher for Leeds. It was an honorary position, given to someone who could be trusted. The Searcher inspected the cloth for sale at the market and rejected anything not considered good enough. It was a way of making sure Leeds only sold high quality cloth, giving it the reputation to surpass other towns.

The Mansion – 1600

The last part. The limewash.

He stood in the yard and watched the workman up on his ladder, working with his trowel to give a smooth finish, brilliant white on the gable above the third storey. The sun came from behind the clouds and caught it, gleaming.

The man kept going, working the same piece over and over until he was satisfied, then climbing back down, slowly. He was a hunched old man, a smock over his clothes, legs bowed with the years, a full beard and a quizzical eye. The best in Leeds, folk said. But the best was what he wanted for this house, so he'd paid the workman his price. It had been worthwhile.

He'd laboured hard enough to afford it, the design in his head for years. Every month he'd counted the coins in the chest, although he already knew exactly how many were there. From his marriage, then the births of Adam and Hannah, the death of his father, he'd wished the time away until today.

There was money in wool these days. Not like the trade from Bristol or Norwich, but enough to give a fair living to a man with enterprise in his heart. Not the way it had been before Henry had taken all the wealth from the churches. He'd heard the tales when he was young, passed on from his grandfather's father. How Kirkstall sold all their wool abroad, precious little for the town.

The workman lowered his ladder and began to clean his tools.

'You've done a good job.'

The man shrugged.

'Just what you paid me to do.' He raised his head. 'It'll last years, will that. A well-built house.' He hoisted the ladder on his shoulder and left.

It was. It ought to be for everything it cost in materials and design. The frontage on Briggate, the gate through to the yard. A house in the latest fashion, each storey jettied out from the one beneath, not only in the front but on the sides. Good mullioned windows to bring in the light, entrances to the yard and the street. Strong hearths for heat and a kitchen to prepare a feast.

With a warehouse for cloth, a strongroom for his accounts and money, and cobbles down over the mud, it was finished. Finally.

He stood by the entrance, gazing across Briggate to the old house. It had been home to the family longer than anyone could recall. Cramped, cold, dark. It was no place for a modern man and his family. When his father died, as soon as the coffin was in the ground, he'd begun to make his plans. His mother would have objected. She'd have talked about the history in the wood, but she'd been gone these twenty years now.

He could hear the children inside, running up and down the staircase. Soon enough he'd go in and tell them to have respect for property. For now they could have their moment of fun.

One long shelf in the warehouse was full, the cloth bundled and tied. Already sold, simply waiting for a boat to carry it down to the coast. There'd be more to take its place. He'd bought lengths at the market on Leeds Bridge two days before. It was off with the fuller now. Dyeing, then stretching on the tenter frames, carefully cropped and ready to go on its way. It took time. Success took patience. His father had drummed that into him. But it needed more than that. An eye for opportunity, the willingness to gamble, to parlay a little into a lot.

He had orders from the Low Counties, down into Italy, all the way to Jamestown in Virginia. A man had to look to new markets. It was how he'd been able to afford this house. Soon others would follow, he'd wager good money on it. Richard Sykes had talked about building when they shared a jug of wine last month. And there was Metcalf, although he probably had even grander visions. The only one who wouldn't was Bowman the shoemaker. He loved that place with its bowed windows for showing off his goods.

Leeds had grown and changed, there was no doubt about it. When he was a lad there'd been nothing to the place, it seemed. Now he saw new faces each day, and more people on the streets than he could count. Folk with money in their purses.

He slapped a hand against the house's corner beam, feeling it solid under his palm. A house to last for years and years. For his children and theirs, and all the generations to come.

Historical note: In Lambert's Yard, just off Lower Briggate (named for the tea merchant who lived there at the end of the 19th century) is the gable end of the oldest house in Leeds. It was built in 1600, a new, impressive house for someone with money. You can still go into the yard, at the side of a restaurant, and see it. Of course, it's changed over the centuries, but this is real living history in front of your eyes. There's been talk of renovation, but at the end of 2014 nothing's been done, sadly.

Walter Calverley – 1605

'He won't plead, my Lord.'

'Have you pressed him?' Baron Cobham asked the gaoler.

'We have, my Lord. See for yourself.' He opened the door to the room. Walter Calverley lay there on the stone floor, wrists and ankles chained so his body made an X. A wooden door had been placed on top of him, piled with rocks.

'You know the law,' Cobham said as he studied Calverley's face. There must have been a hundredweight on top of him, but he didn't show any pain. Just the fire of fury in his eyes. 'He's a lunatic. Press him until he says he's guilty or not. He's killed two of his children and came damn close to murdering his wife, too. He'd have had the last boy if the villagers hadn't caught him. Press him.'

'Yes, my Lord,' the gaoler said as the Baron walked away along the corridor of York Castle.

It hadn't always been this way, Walter Calverley thought. He hadn't always been a madman, had he? He could remember times when he'd been happy. Back when he'd been young, and the grounds of the Old Hall in Calverley seemed to stretch forever. But then, back in '72, his father had died and the world seemed to slow as it span around the sun.

Walter inherited the titles: the squire of six manors, in Fagley, Farsley, Bolton, Burley-in Wharfedale, Eccleshill, and Seacroft. He'd learned them like a rhyme. They were his, but he was too young to understand what that meant. He had money, his mother said. But he'd always had money, never wanted for anything. He had responsibilities, but what were they? He didn't know, and when they tried to tell him, he no longer cared. A cup or two of wine, maybe more, a good game of cards; that was the life.

It stayed that way when he went to Cambridge in May of '79. He met good fellows there, carousers all of them. The days for sleeping, the nights for pleasure. Exactly how it should be for a young man.

But it palled quickly enough, and by October he was back in

Calverley, much to the displeasure of his guardian, Baron Cobham.

It was there he met Catherine. The same name as his mother. A sweet, pretty girl. How had he never seen her before? Her father's farm backed on to the grounds of the hall. She was a girl with a winsome face and a gentle manner, the kind for love, not sport. And in her he believed he saw someone who could change him for the better. He asked her to marry him and she agreed.

That all changed with Cobham's summons to London. The note was curt, but Walter knew he had to obey. Cobham held the purse strings and decided how much money he could receive until he came of age.

Nigh on a week's journey until he was in the house on Thames Street, the capital a bustle of noise and sounds and smells around him. The garden ran down to the river, masts ranged like a forest on the water.

'Write to her,' Cobham ordered him. 'She does read, doesn't she?'

'Of course.'

'Tell her it's over, that on reflection she's not suitable.'

'I love her.'

Cobham's stare was cold.

'What does that matter? If you love her, take her on the side once you're properly wed. Marriage is for gain and bringing heirs into the world. If you want passion, find it in the arms of a whore. You're here because you have a duty to do. Or would you rather starve until you're twenty-one?'

He had him by the ballocks, and Walter knew it. He was weak. He sent the letter that night.

'Here's the girl you're going to marry.' Cobham nodded and the servant opened the door to usher in a girl with an eager, curdled gaze.

'Philippa. Meet the man who'll be your husband.' Walter stood and bowed. 'Walter, this is my granddaughter, Philippa Brooke. I've considered it all, and this will be a good match for you both. And when you marry, boy, control of all the estates will become yours.'

All his. All gone now.

They'd read the banns that first Sunday in London, and the two that came after, and then the wedding. A dazzling affair. But the problems began as soon as they came north, to the Old Hall. It was uncivilised up here, she complained.

Her tongue was as sharp as any knife and it never ceased. Every little thing had to be picked apart, until he stormed out, down to the inn, to dice and drink. Sometimes into Leeds for company. Once, out hawking, he saw Catherine riding with a man. She had a new suitor, he'd heard. Rage rose in him like water in a vessel. He could have been happy with her if he'd stood his ground, but he didn't have any courage. He spurred the horse and galloped to the inn, drinking himself insensible.

He did his duty and produced heirs, bawling, puking boys to take his place in time: William, Walter and Henry. The nursemaid cared for them. Dutifully she presented them for his inspection. William was four, polite and fearful to the point of annoyance. Walter not old enough to speak yet, just a year and a half, and Henry out with the wet nurse in the village.

And the money? That was all gone, not that there ever was as much as he'd imagined. Cobham had had his hands in the fortune, he was sure of that. It was the man's way. But with a wife and three brats, as well as his own pleasure and the expenses of the estates, the coffers were bare.

He lived on credit, and soon enough there'd be no more of that.

There were days he'd walk out of the Old Hall, climb to the top of the moor, where none could see or hear him, and scream until his voice was hoarse. It was the only way to take the pressure from his mind, to stop feeling as if his head would explode as his problems crowded around him.

Then, once he was home, Philippa would ask where he'd been. Questions, accusations. She loved him no more than he loved her. But where he wanted none of her, she used every word as a dagger to slit his skin.

St George's Day. The village taking the holiday and celebrating. Walter had been up an hour, his head pounding from the drink of the night before, when the servant showed in the messenger. Three letters, two of them from creditors to toss on the fire.

The last from his cousin, Mark. He'd been at Cambridge with Mark's brother, Richard. As good a man as ever lived, a drinker, a man to wager and whore with at night.

News, cousin, and bad tidings at that: Richard has been taken by the law and put in prison for a debt at Cambridge. Six pounds. Our father won't pay it, saying Richard can rot in gaol for a year. I have no money, save what my father gives me. So I have to look to his friends on his behalf...

Walter tore it up and threw it into the flames. He could no more help Richard than he could help himself. And he knew the debt. He knew it well. It was his. Signing for food and drink and new suits of clothes in Richard's name. A joke. It had seemed a good one at the time, with no thought of consequence.

He couldn't raise that amount, not now. His life was broken and others were paying the price.

He drank steadily, all through the day. The only person he'd allow in the room was his servant, bringing more wine, ale, brandy, whatever was in the house. When Philippa tried to enter he threw a piece of plate at her head, ranting and raging.

It was all her fault. If he could have married Catherine, she could have saved him. He'd have known the happiness he'd experienced when he was young and life was just innocence and simple fun.

By evening he had his plan. He'd sweep away this life, destroy it. Make himself clean again. He'd go to Catherine and beg her. Ask for his salvation.

With his dagger in his hand, Walter climbed the stair. He threw the door of the nursery open. Walter and William asleep in their beds, so easy to kill. Five thrusts each, his tears coming as he did it. Tears of joy. Tears of freedom.

He was striding back along the corridor when Philippa came out of her room, hair down, wearing her nightgown, a shawl gathered around her shoulders. He struck at her, seeing her blood run, hearing her cry out.

Outside, in the stable, he saddled his favourite mare. One more thing to do until he was clean again, until he could make his fresh start with Catherine. He galloped out of the gate, spirits soaring for the first time since he'd put the ring on the woman's finger.

The word passed faster than he could ride. In the darkness he lost his path twice, tracking back. The village with Henry and his wet nurse was no more than a mile, but he was damned if he could find it in the night. And when he did come to the right track, the village men were waiting, dragging him off the horse and taking him to the magistrate.

Murder, they called it, and carried him off to gaol. Not even to Leeds, but all the way to Wakefield.

And now it was August, hot even in the depths of York Castle. He lay, listening, and the gaoler asked him once more how he wanted to plead, before he added another stone. But what the man didn't understand was that every weight on his chest took the load from his heart. And once his chest was crushed and all the life was gone, well, then he'd find his freedom. At last.

Historical Note: The facts of this tale are true, and Walter Calverley was pressed to death on the orders of the Star Chamber after he refused to plead on the killings of two of his sons and the wounding of his wife. By then he was in debt, and the letter saying an old friend was in jail for a debt of Walter's, dating back to his student days, seems to have finally turned his mind. He died in York on August 5, 1605. There are claims that his ghost can be seen at night, riding a black horse and waving a bloodstained dagger, on the lanes around St. Wilfrid's Church in Calverley, where he's buried.

The Marvellous Doors of Mr. Harrison - 1626

'Sir?' The carpenter frowned as he spoke, as if the request had made no sense. He wiped some sawdust from the hairs on his brawny forearm as he waited to hear it again.

John Harrison smiled patiently.

'I'd like you to cut holes in the bottom of each door in the house,' he repeated. 'They haven't been hung yet, have they?'

'Well, no, sir,' the carpenter agreed. It was obvious, after all. Each doorway in this new house was empty, the finished items out in the courtyard, covered with canvas in case of rain. He'd been planning to start putting them up after his dinner. But why someone would want to cut holes in perfectly good oak, he really didn't know.

'They don't need to be large holes,' Harrison continued, as if it was the most reasonable thing in the world. 'Just about this wide and this tall.' He held his hands apart to offer an idea of the size. 'Can you do that, please?'

'I can,' the carpenter allowed slowly, rubbing at the bristles on his chin. He'd been working with wood for thirty years, ever since he was a lad, and no one had asked him this before. He was a craftsman, a master at his trade, a guild member. To be asked to saw holes in work he'd completed seemed wrong. He could carve a bannister so smooth against the fingers that it felt like holding silk. He could polish wood so clear that it shone as brightly as any mirror. He took pride in everything he did. But this? Where was the sense in it?

It offended him, although he was careful not to show it. Not when the man staring at him so hopefully was the richest man in Leeds, the man who'd been paying his wages for months – and generous wages they were, too, he'd admit – as he helped shape the house.

Mr. Harrison had never seemed to be a strange one. A generous soul, yes. He'd inherited plenty of money and made even more as a cloth merchant. He'd paid for a market cross for the town, the one that stood near the top of Briggate. He'd given land for the new Grammar School in that field past the Head Row, which was fine for those who wanted to learn reading and writing and all the things the gentry needed. But it was like everyone said, he had so much money and property that he'd never even miss a hundred pounds.

'I can do it,' he allowed slowly. It would mean more work.

His apprentices had cut and shaped the doors. He'd inspected their work, corrected their errors and boxed them round the ears for stupid mistakes. Each one had beautiful panels, dark and lovely. He'd selected the wood himself, sensing how easily they'd work and the way they'd hold their colour once he'd finished with them. As they were they had balance and proportion, all the things he valued. And now he was being asked to ruin that. He shook his head slightly.

'Is something wrong, Master Cockcroft?' Harrison asked worriedly. He had a lively face, the hair receding along his scalp, with dark, arching eyebrows and a moustache that fluttered as he talked. He was as impeccably dressed as ever, his neckband a starched, brilliant while, his black velvet doublet without a smudge of dirt.

'No, sir, nothing wrong at all.' He gazed around the room, up on the second storey of the house. It looked down on Briggate and out along Boar Lane, a handsome bedroom that would claim the light at the shank of the day. The floorboards were even, fitted together so well that he could just slide a fingernail between them. The mullions on the windows gleamed. It was a beautiful room.

But the whole house suited a man of position, and Harrison certainly had that. The courtyard was cobbled, the warehouse for cloth standing at the other side, and beyond that the garden, fruit trees already planted to make an orchard. It had cost the man a pretty penny and it wasn't finished yet. It might never be if he kept making ridiculous requests like this.

'Thank you,' Harrison said with a smile and a nod. 'My wife and I talked about it and decided it was the best solution.'

That explained it, Cockcroft thought. Women. Marriage. He had no calling to it himself, he was happier by himself, with a housekeeper to keep the place tidy and feed the 'prentices. Women did odd things to a man's mind. And Harrison and Mrs. Elizabeth, they'd been together a good twenty years by now, probably more. By now she'd addled his brain if he was coming up with ideas like this.

He'd set the apprentices to work in the morning. The job was simple enough, to measure and cut, then smooth and finish the wood.

'All the doors, sir?' he asked. With front and back there had to be close to fifteen of them.

'Not the front door,' Harrison answered with a quick laugh, then considered. 'And perhaps not the rear door, either. After all, we don't want to let in draughts, do we?'

'Of course not.' That was something, he thought. At least none of the passers-by would see what he'd been made to do to his doors. He wouldn't be reminded of it every time he walked past. It was unlikely that anyone he knew would be invited inside. He'd make sure the apprentices didn't tell anyone, swear them to it. With a little luck word wouldn't spread around town and he wouldn't be the butt of jokes.

'Right.' Harrison rubbed his pale hands together. 'That's settled. Won't be long before we can move in, eh?'

'Another week, I think, sir.' It wouldn't take that long, of course. But over the years he'd learned to say this. Unless something he couldn't imagine happened, like being asked to cut holes in walls or ceilings, he should be done in three days. Then another day to pad out the bill a little and he'd say he was finished. Mr. Harrison would be happy he'd completed everything early, and he'd be a little fatter in the purse when the account was settled. Everyone would be happy.

'Excellent news, Mr. Cockcroft. Excellent.' He shook the carpenter's right hand and pumped it. 'Thank you once more for this.' He turned to leave.

'Mr Harrison, sir,' Cockcroft said to his back. 'Just one question, if I may.'

The merchant turned back, cocking his head quizzically.

'Of course.'

'Why do you want holes in all them doors, anyway?'

'Ah. It's for the cats, Mr. Cockcroft, the cats. We have five of them and they hate to be confined in one room. So my wife came up with this solution to let them wander where they will. I think it's a wonderful idea, don't you?' He gave a small bow. 'And now I'll wish you good day.'

Historical Note: Several people have been great benefactors to Leeds, but John Harrison was the first. In the first half of the 17th century, he paid for a market cross, built St. John's Church (which still stands on New Briggate) and Harrison's almshouses, gave land and paid for the building of the Grammar School where the Grand Theatre now stands, and more. He inherited money and made more in the wool trade. There's also a story concerning him, Charles I and a tankard full of gold coins. He did build a house in town that stood around a courtyard; by the 1700s it was an inn. As to the doors, it's Thoresby who relates that tale. Is it true? Perhaps. But it's a good tale, which can sometimes be more important than fact.

Little Alice Musgrove – 1645

Little Alice Musgrave, lying in her bed,
Little Alice Musgrave with plague in her head,
All the prayers for Alice that all the preachers said,
Little Alice Musgrave, buried and dead.

The children sang it for years afterwards, long after most people had forgotten who Alice had even been alive. At first I chased them away and cuff at their heads, yelling through my tears, shouting at them to shut up. But it didn't help. They'd keep on singing and every word cut deeper and deeper into my heart until I couldn't cry out any more.

Last week I heard it again. A pair of girls, neither of them more than six, were using it as a rhyme for skipping ropes. The good Lord alone knows where they'd learned it. Alice has been dead these twenty years now. Maybe they'd heard their mother idly singing a memory one day.

I was walking along Call Lane with my granddaughter, her hand tight in mine, and the words just made me stop, frozen as winter. I thought my heart might never beat again.

'What is it, Grandmama?' Emily asked. 'Why are you crying like that?'

I had to draw in my breath slowly before I could answer her.

'It's nothing, child,' I told her. 'Just a dream that flew past.' I tried to make my voice light but it was filled with the weight of all the tears I'd cried. 'Come on, let's get ourselves home. Mama will be wondering where we are.' I clutched her hand tighter and we hurried away.

It wouldn't go away. In the darkness, when I lay alone on the sheet and straw, it came back, singing and taunting. It was as if God wasn't going to give me the peace of forgetting, as if He'd uncovered all the jagged edges of memory again.

The Roundheads had come again the year before, so loud that we cowered in the house and prayed they wouldn't come in and kill us. But Leeds had been buffeted like a feather in the wind, from King to Parliament and back again, more dead each time.

But these troops stayed. It felt like a year of mud, when every colour was brown or black and the rains just came and came. The men put up notices for everything – church attendance, how we had to behave, what we could wear. They forbade us from celebrating the birth of our Lord in the old way. That was sinful, they said.

We'd been poor before, desperate for every penny and every bite. But now they took all our joy, too. Snow fell to bring in the New Year, only the pikemen with their shining leather boots and glittering weapons allowed on the streets after dark.

We tried to make ourselves into mice, scurrying and unnoticed lest the cat see us and pounce. Sometimes they'd come and drag one of the menfolk away with their accusations of supporting the king. If he ever came home again it was as someone broken and quiet.

I feared for my husband. He'd been a clerk to lawyer Bolton before the attorney had fled. Now Bolton's grand house on Briggate was a ruin, a burned-out gap in the street and there was a fine waiting against his name. I kept thinking they'd arrived one day and take Roger off.

He had no work. No one needed a man with his letters. The law was whatever the soldiers said, not something to be argued in a courtroom or written into books. And the cloth trade had dwindled so far that even some of the merchants went hungry. Once it would have been a marvel to see a grand man begging his bread. Now it happened every day.

We had three girls to feed, Alice, Hannah and Anne. They often went hungry, but we fed them before we took anything to eat. When Alice woke in the night, moaning with pain, at first I thought it was nothing more than an empty belly.

'Hush, love,' I whispered. 'Just go back to sleep now.'

But she didn't stop.

'It hurts, mama.'

I knelt by the bed she shared with her sisters, just a sheet over old straw. Her skin was so hot I thought it could burn my fingers and her shift was soaked with sweat. I bathed her face with cold water and stroked her damp hair, softly singing every lullaby I could remember. And I prayed. The first of so many prayers to rise from Leeds that year, but God blocked His ear to them all.

By morning she was cold, shaking and shivering with it. Nothing I did could help. I sent Roger to bring the wise woman who lived on Kirkgate. She looked, poking my beautiful little girl with her fingers so that she gave a scream like Christ's agony.

Outside, where a bitter wind came out of the west, the woman put her arms on my shoulders and looked at me with her ancient eyes.

'She has the pestilence,' she said softly.

I opened my mouth. I wanted to say no, to shout, to cry, but nothing came. All I could think was why was He judging her like this? What had she done? She was only eleven, she had no sins to her name.

'I'll bring something in a little while,' the woman continued. 'It'll help her rest and ease the pain a little.' Then she was gone and I was out there, alone as the cold whipped around me.

The word passed quickly, as if the wind had carried it around the town. The soldiers' doctor arrived in his neat, clean uniform to examine her then shake his head. A pair of troopers were placed outside our door to keep folk away. We were trapped inside. Roger tried to amuse Hannah and Anne, to distract them, while I tended to Alice. The wise woman delivered her little bottle, something clear and sweet-smelling inside, and it worked. My beautiful girl slept. *Little Alice Musgrave with plague in her head.* But it was on her body, the lumps growing so quickly under her arms and between her legs, the stink growing stronger with every hour, as if death was consuming her inch by inch.

The army left food outside our door, kindling and blankets. For the first time in a year we could have lived like human beings if we'd wanted. But who could have an appetite with this? I tried to keep Alice warm when the cold racked her, hugging her close to give her my heat. Weariness took me deep into my bones but I couldn't sleep. I only had hours left with my daughter and I couldn't let any moment of them slip away.

They held a service in St. John's to pray for her, I heard later. For her soul and her salvation. What good is that when the Lord has turned away, I wanted to shout? But I never said a word.

After a day she'd moved beyond speech, only able to make noises like a baby, each one full of pain and fright. Her swellings turned black, the change coming in the blink of an eye. I kept hold of her hand, letting her know that we all loved her. All I wanted now was for her suffering to end.

Alice lasted until the shank of the day. She wasn't fighting, not even aware, just waiting. Then she gulped in a breath and it was over. I sat, still clutching her fingers and felt life leave her.

They took her body away quickly, the first to go into a plague pit. No coffin, no more than a winding sheet and a covering of quicklime. They wouldn't let us go to watch her being placed in the earth. All we were allowed were the four walls of our room and a heaven full of sorrow in our hearts.

Two mornings later it was Roger who began to sweat and by dinner Hannah was ill. I tended to them as best I could, moving like a ghost from one to the other as Anne became a silent, frightened child in the corner, too scared to move in case death caught her.

I hadn't had time to grieve for my Alice when the others fell ill. All I could do was exist, snatch rest when I could, lying next to a body with the stench of decay, waking to another scream or a moan.

At least He took them quickly, less than a day each. And then it was just Anne and I, waiting and wondering how long before it came for us, too.

But it never happened. After a week I walked outside. People talked and went about their business, trying to pretend nothing had occurred, as if Alice and Roger and Hannah hadn't died. Yet I could see the terror in their eyes and the way they shunned me; I carried the pestilence like a shadow around me. Then I heard the rhyme for the first time, a group of children playing down the road, throwing a ball from one to the other. *Little Alice Musgrave, lying in her bed.* I ran towards them screaming and saw them scatter in surprise. My arm caught one boy and I started to hit him over and over as the tears tumbled down my cheeks.

Spring came, sunny, bright and fertile to mock us all. I knew what it meant. With the warm weather the plague would remain in Leeds. While others held their Bibles close, I prayed it would take me and Anne, that it would lift the weight in our hearts. Each week there'd be fewer faces I knew on the streets, but death kept denying me.

The soldiers left in the end. I'd lost track of how long they stayed; sometimes it seemed as if they'd always been there. Now we have a king again in London, or so they say. It makes little difference to our life here.

The houses that were destroyed have been rebuilt. Maybe they're even grander than they were before, I can't remember. My Anne is married with a little girl of her own. She had one before but Alice died when she was no more than a month old. I tried to tell her it was a fated name, but she wouldn't listen to me.

I play with Emily, take her to the market and down to the river where men sell the fish they catch. I live with them, accompany them to church on a Sunday, but all I pray for now is to forget.

Historical Note: Leeds changed hands several times during the first English Civil War, but by 1645 it had been under the control of a garrison of Parliament troops for several months. Many Royalist supporters had fled. Others, many of them merchants, were being investigated and crippling fines would be levied on them. The town was in steep decline when a case of plague was reported in March, a girl named Alice Musgrave, just eleven years old, who lived on Vicar Lane, one of the poorest areas. She was the first victim, but she certainly wouldn't be the last. By the end of the year, when the plague had run its course, the roll of the dead contained 1,325 names, around one-third of the population of Leeds.

Mr. Thoresby and the Water Engine – 1694

Ralph Thoresby leaned heavily on his walking stick as he peered into the trench. He stood for a full minute, inspecting the labourers as they dug along Kirkgate.

He was a rotund man, but still robust, dressed in a coat of good, heavy wool, carefully cut to show off his heavily embroidered waistcoat. His legs were stout, strong from all the years of walking around Leeds and the country that surrounded it. The area was his passion and his learning. And now he was alive to see a remarkable thing: running water coming to the houses of the town. He amended the thought: it would go to the houses that could afford to subscribe to the service.

Finally, satisfied, he stood upright, pushing the full periwig back over his shoulders and strode away down Briggate, with greetings and nods to everyone he knew – so many people were crammed into Leeds these days, it seemed. More of them every week, pushed into the little courts that had grown higgledy-piggledy off either side of Briggate. He stopped, took a battered notebook and pencil from one of the large pockets in the waistcoat and scribbled a line or two before carrying on.

He knew exactly where he was going, to the new brick building that had gone up next to Leeds Bridge. Without knocking, he entered, surprising the two men standing at a table and poring over a set of plans. Close by, beyond a door, he could hear others hammering and swearing, and the heavy, ringing sound of metal being inched into place.

'Good day to you both,' Thoresby said as they stared at him. 'Would one of you be Mr. Sorocold?'

'I am,' the smaller man replied. His face had a serious expression, almost stern, with thin lips and a beady gaze. His coat and breeches were plain cloth, everything unadorned, heavy woollen stockings vanishing into thick boots. 'How may I help you, Mr..?'

'Mr. Thoresby.' He extended his hand eagerly. 'Ralph Thoresby. I've been eager to meet you, sir. You're doing wonderful things for this town. But I have a question or two, if you'd be so good as to indulge me.'

'Of course,' Sorocold agreed reluctantly. He glanced at his companion and gave a small shrug. 'Carry on with that for the moment,' he instructed. 'Now sir, what can I do for you?'

'I'd like to see this remarkable machine you've created.'

'It's not finished yet,' Sorocold told him. 'I'm sure you've noticed that we're still digging to put the pipes in place. You're a subscriber to the water service?'

'Of course, of course,' Thoresby said with a wide smile. 'Imagine, water running into the house, to turn on and off at will. We live in wonderful times, sir.'

'Ingenious times, Mr. Thoresby.'

'Perhaps you'd be willing to explain it all. If you have the time, of course.'

'I can spare a few minutes,' Sorocold said after a little thought. 'Come with me.'

He led Thoresby to a small platform outside the building, just a few yards from the bridge.

'Look down there,' he said. 'You can see where we draw the water in from the river.'

Two wide metal pipes that protruded into the current.

'You can take in enough with just those?' Thoresby asked in astonishment.

'Indeed, sir, indeed,' Sorocold replied with satisfaction. 'Everything has been finely calculated. To the last gallon. From there the engine will pump the water to the reservoir.'

'I've seen it. At the top of Briggate. But the power to push it that far…'

'Everything calculated and calibrated,' Sorocold assured him again. 'An elevation of ninety feet from the river, with all of Leeds below it. From there the water only has to roll back downhill to the houses.' He smiled at his little joke. 'We use lead pipes to carry the water along the streets to the houses where you have your taps. Everything is progressing very quickly.'

'I was just watching your men work.' Thoresby stood, surveying the Aire. 'Things still trouble me, though,' he said. 'Greatly trouble me.'

Sorocold was curious now.

'What things might they be?'

'Ten years ago this river froze hard in the winter.' He indicated it with a sweep of his stick. 'As far as you can see, up and down. Thick enough for us to hold an ice fair.' He paused and stared at the other man. 'You're from Derby, I believe, Mr. Sorocold?'

'I am.' He acknowledge the fact with a nod of his head.

'Perhaps your rivers don't freeze there. But in Leeds they do. What happens then? How will we have water? The pumps in the street ran deep enough that we had water to drink, but it was cold.'

He shuddered at the memory. 'Bitter cold. And it will happen again. I keep records of the temperature each day. Believe me, sir, it will happen again.'

'If it does, then we will have to shut down,' Sorocold acknowledged amiably. 'There are some things beyond our grasp at the moment. But that will change in time.'

Thoresby nodded.

'Another question, if I might.'

'Of course.'

'The water that runs in these pipes under our streets. Won't that freeze in the winter? And when it does, won't it burst all the pipes?'

'Are you familiar with the idea of the frost line, Mr. Thoresby?'

'No sir, I'm not. No more than an idea of it.'

'The frost will only go so deep into the earth,' Sorocold explained. 'The edge of that penetration is called the frost line. Below that the ground stays warm enough for the water to remain liquid. We put our pipes below that frost line. So the pipes shouldn't freeze or burst.'

In the end they talked for another hour. The chill October wind picked up, but neither man seemed to notice, engrossed in their conversation. Sorocold had a sharp mind, Thoresby decided approvingly. Not just an engineer but a man of some learning. A scientist. As a Fellow of the Royal Society, that left him happy. A like mind in Leeds, even if the man would only remain until the water engine was running smoothly.

Before he left, Thoresby said:

'I'd call it a great favour if you'd come to my house on Kirkgate sometime, sir. I have some curiosities in my museum that might interest you.'

'Do you?' Sorocold was intrigued.

'I do, sir!' Thoresby beamed. 'Not only the coins that my father collected, ones that date back to when the Romans lived in these lands, but the things I've acquired. I have the foot of a white bear, manuscripts in church Latin, a bow from India, even a piece of amber that holds a fly intact, if you can believe that, sir. Remarkable things. I'd be honoured if you were my guest for dinner one day so I could show you properly.' The bell at the Parish Church tolled the hour. Nine o'clock. 'Now I've kept you long enough, I'm afraid. Soon, sir, present yourself at my house soon. Thoresby on Kirkgate.

Everyone knows where I am.' And with a short bow he was gone.

He roamed back up Briggate with a smile on his face. An excellent encounter. Lost in thought, he passed the tiny entrances that led to the courts where the poor lived. By the Moot Hall, which stood like an island in the middle of the street, Thoresby took the right fork, but scarcely noticed the overwhelming stench of the Shambles, with the butchers selling their meat and crying their goods.

He crossed the Head Row, then stopped at the edge of a large hole in the ground close by St. John's Church. This would become the reservoir for the water. Once it was filled, of course, he told himself. Gazing back down towards the river, he still found the idea strange, hard to believe. But Sorocold had made it all seem so sensible. So natural and ordered. Man in control of the elements.

A series of lead pipes lay a third of the way up the hole, some higher than the others. The lower ones transported the water from the reservoir to the subscribers, the engineer had told him. Those higher up brought the water from the river. It was clever, it was intelligent. And he knew it would work. He'd already proved the efficacy of it all elsewhere.

The church bell brought him back to the world. Half past the hour. He ought to return home. For the first time that morning he felt the cold in the wind, slicing through his clothes like a knife. Thoresby shivered. The servants would have dinner ready for ten, as they always did, and his wife would be expecting him.

Besides, he had things that he needed to do at home. More work on his book, his history of Leeds. Two hours of research and writing in the afternoon. There was more he needed to check for the section on the Killingbeck family and still he couldn't determine if the old stories of Penda being killed in battle at Grimes Dyke were true, or simply tales people told round their fires. He needed to discover the truth of the matter.

'So much to know,' he said to himself as he turned and walked away.

Down near the corner of Kirkgate it seemed as if half the road had been excavated. A man was gently coaxing a horse into dragging a heavy lead pipe towards the deep hole. Fascinated, Thoresby stood and watched until the pipe rolled down the gentle slope into the earth and a group of labours followed quickly to manhandle it into place.

'Is this for the water?' he asked the foreman.

'It is that, sir,' the man replied and smiled to show three

teeth left in his mouth. 'Going at a cracking pace, it is, too. At this rate we'll be done in a month.'

He watched for a full minute more, then turned for home. A thought came to him: Why did every improvement in Leeds involve digging up the streets? For cobbles, for new houses, for every little thing, it seemed. He made a quick note of it before he opened the door to his house.

In the hearth of the dining room, the fire was roaring, warm and welcoming. He hung his hat on the hook and put his stick in the stand then walked into the room to stand near the blaze rubbing his hands.

His wife sat at the table.

'Did you go out without a greatcoat again?' she asked kindly.

'I did,' he admitted. 'But it's not too chilly outside.'

'You'll catch your death of cold,' she warned him.

Thoresby smiled.

'But I've learned wonderful things, my dear. Wonderful things!'

Historical Note: Ralph Thoresby is famous for his book, *Ducatus Leodiensis*, published in 1715. It's a history of Leeds and the areas, as well as the great families of the district. In October 1694 he noted in his diary that they were digging to lay the pipes for water to the homes of those who subscribed to the new service. George Sorocold was the engineer who devised and supervised bringing running water to Leeds, with the water engine just by Leeds Bridge. Even now, if you look just to the east of the bridge, at the waterline, you can still see the holes for the intake pipes.

Mr. Thoresby's Curiosities – 1725

'It won't do,' he said, shaking his head and pursing his lips. 'It just won't do.'

'No, sir,' I agreed.

Mr. Brocklehurst looked slowly around the room once more. He'd tied his stock too tightly in the morning and his large face had been red all day.

'No,' he repeated. 'It just won't do.'

But it would have to be done. Every item in this collection of curiosities needed to be catalogued. And I knew it wouldn't fall to Brocklehurst the lawyer to do it. It would be my job, his clerk.

Mr. Thoresby had amassed thousands upon thousands of objects during his life, so many that he'd needed to build an annexe to this modest house on Kirkgate for them all. Now he'd passed on his heirs needed an inventory of everything.

I'd miss the man. He'd been my favourite of Mr. Brocklehurst's clients. Whenever he'd visit the office he asked after my wife and children with honest interest. No matter that he was a gentleman with his independent means and I was no more than a law clerk.

Even after his first stroke his mind had been alert. I'd come here several times with papers to be signed and he'd always been polite. He'd even insisted on showing me around this place, his *museum* as he called it with a wry little smile, and he'd pressed a copy of his book on me, his history of Leeds and the areas around it, picking it from a tall pile, blowing off the dust and inscribing it with his name, writing in an awkward scrawl. I didn't have the heart to tell him that only gentlemen had the leisure for reading and learning. For the rest of us, life was made for work and sleep. So his *Ducatus Leodiensis* propped up a broken table leg in our house now, the gold letters on the spine growing dirtier each month.

Brocklehurst paced around the room, hands clasped together in the small of his back, pausing here and there to look at this and that. Finally he announced:

'Well, you'd better get to work. And don't be too long about it. I want you back in the office as soon as possible. There's plenty of work among the living.'

'Yes, sir.' I opened the ledger on an old desk then set down the quill and the ink pot, hearing the door slam in the empty house as the lawyer left. I knew I should begin the task, but instead I walked to a shelf at the far end of the room and picked up a small object.

I'd last been here two months earlier, no more than a fortnight before Mr. Thoresby suffered his second stroke and died. I'd come on a trifling errand, his signature on a note to append to an annuity. He'd been sitting in his parlour, lost in thought when I was shown through.

'Young man,' he said with real pleasure, as if I'd been his first visitor in an age. He struggled to his feet with the help of a stick, putting out a heavy, palsied hand to grip mine. Wigless, he showed wisps of grey hair over a shiny pink skull, and a mouth that drooped on one side. But his eyes still twinkled. Over the last months he'd grown portly, his movements confined to his house or the streets close by. No more wanderings around England or setting off in the morning to walk to York and dine with the archbishop. An invalid now, his wide world had become so small. 'Come with me, come on. I have something very special to show you,' he urged, his voice just an echo of the cannon boom it had once been.

I followed him through to this room of wonders. He shuffled slowly, pausing two or three times to catch his breath. Yet once we reached the shelf and he reached out, it was as if his illness had never happened. His hand was steady as a youth's and his thick sausage fingers were deft as he plucked up the item.

'Do you see that?' he asked me, letting it sit on his palm. 'The vicar in Rothwell sent it to me last week.' He displayed it like something precious but I had no idea what it could be. I wasn't like him, I had no knowledge of these things, no chance to learn. My only schooling had been letters and numbers before I had to earn my way in the world. It seemed nothing more than a piece of sharp stone, how could it have value? He saw my look and smiled. 'Would you like me to tell you?'

'Yes, sir, I would.' If it was important to him then it must have a purpose, I thought.

'Long ago, before there was any Cambodunum, or Leodis or Leeds, long before anyone thought of a town here, there were people in this country,' he began. It wasn't the chiding, strident tone of my old schoolmaster. Instead, there was enjoyment in his voice sharing these things with all the eagerness of an enthusiast.

'Where did they live?' I wondered.

'In caves, perhaps, or out in the open. We don't know that yet,' he answered with a small sigh, as if he was disappointed that he'd never learn. 'But they hunted. They had to, for food. And they possessed spears and arrows, we do know that. And clubs, I suppose,' he added, as if it was an aside to himself. 'This, young man, is an arrowhead made of flint.'

Once he told me, I could discern the shape of it, the point at one end. It was delicate, crude yet carefully worked and I marvelled at how anyone could have made that so long ago and that it could still be found like this.

'Just imagine,' Mr. Thoresby continued, 'that a man might have killed many animals with this arrow. Perhaps it ended up in some beast that escaped him. Or maybe it was a wild shot he never found again. Or,' he winked at me, 'he might simply have lost it somewhere.'

He replaced the arrowhead on the shelf and we returned to the parlour to finish our business. Since then I'd thought of it often. I told my wife about it but she paid it little mind. Seeing an arrowhead wouldn't put food on our table or clothe our children. It came to me later that I'd never asked him just how old it was. He would have known; after all, he was acknowledged to be the wisest man in Leeds. Now, though, he was interred under the choir of the Parish Church, his widow gone to live with one of their sons.

I lifted the arrowhead very carefully, astonished that something with all this weight of years on it could be so light. I ran my thumb along the edge and gasped out loud to discover it was still sharp enough to cut the skin. How long had it taken to fashion something like this? What tools had he used? Suddenly I had so many questions ringing like Sunday morning bells in my head and no one to answer them.

Furtively I looked around, as if there might be someone spying on me. It was a ridiculous fancy, of course. The house was all closed up, the shutters pulled tight, the air inside stuffy, still holding that old, desperate smell of disease and death that tugged at the nostrils. Then I took out my kerchief and gently wrapped it around the arrowhead. Another glance over my shoulder and I tucked it away in my coat pocket. No one would know. No one but me would count all the curiosities here.

Historical Note: It would be impossible to have something claiming to represent Leeds without including Ralph Thoresby in some way. He was a truly remarkable man, one of those amateurs who don't exist anymore, with a mind that was curious about everything. He did have a museum at his house, filled with all manner of items, and so large that he needed an annexe to house it. He died in 1725, ten years after publishing *Ducatus Leodiensis*, his definitive history of

Leeds and the areas around it, still a vital work of history. A few decades later his collection, part of which he inherited from his father, was auctioned off. These days his memory is honoured by the Thoresby society – the local history society – and a blue plaque where his house once stood on Kirkgate.

Remember, Remember- 1745

He fitted the new string on the fiddle and tightened the peg slowly, plucking it over and over as his wrist turned the tuner until it was close to a G. It would keep going flat during the evening and he'd have to re-tune, but it couldn't be helped. At least it was the bottom string; he'd just try and use it as little as possible.

'Are you ready, Joshua Walker?' Toby called from outside the door.

'Aye,' he said. 'Ready and willing.'

By eight, all the bonfires were burning well, sparks rising up into the darkness, people drinking and passing around the jugs of ale from one person to the next. Josh Walker locked the fiddle away in his room, safe from harm.

In the end it had all gone well. The string had been fair with him, staying in tune until the new piece had been performed, then all through the procession from the Assembly Room up to the big fire on the open ground across from St. John's. He'd been paid and given his share of scraps from the banquet, enough to feed him for a day if he was careful.

He walked up Briggate, the cudgel swinging from his wrist, eyes alert. It was a night for celebration, one where folk stayed out late, even the children. But who wouldn't want to remember someone trying to blow up Parliament and all those down in London who only cared for themselves? Even if the plotters were all Papists, they'd done something right.

He rubbed the sleeve of his heavy greatcoat over the Town Waits badge, seeing it shine in the light from the bonfire. He was proud of that. It meant he made his living from the fiddle. Well, that and being part of the night watch, but he'd never heard of anyone earning enough money just from music.

After five years of doing this he knew what to expect. The apprentices would have their plans, staying out long after good folk were off to their beds. They'd be looking for a fight and before it was all done the night watch would give them one. There'd be some broken heads and a few waking up in gaol. The new gaol, they still called it, although it had been built before he was born.

They needed to learn some fresh tunes before Christmas, he thought. It was always a busy season, a time to line the pockets by playing balls and parties all over town. Last year they'd been invited out to Temple Newsam, the year before as far as Harrogate. He'd made enough to buy a new dress for his wife and clothes for his children. Roger was five and he'd just started the lad playing the fiddle, some simple fingering and learning how to hold it, exactly the way his own father had taught him.

He didn't read music, none of the Waits did, but he had a quick ear. All he needed was to listen to something twice and he could play it, every note perfect. The others would pick it up from him and within half an hour they'd have it arranged and ready to perform. There was a melody he'd had in his head for days, one that wouldn't go away. Josh was still trying to decide if he'd heard it somewhere or if it was a gift from God. He hummed it as he walked.

So far it had all been quiet. Several people had shot off muskets and fowling pieces, but no one had been hurt. No children had fallen into the flames, there hadn't been any fights... all the trouble would happen later, once the families had drifted away. And it would come, it did every year. But then they'd be ready for it. This year, perhaps, the apprentices would at least manage to hit the statue of Queen Anne with their stones, unless they were already too drunk.

He stood close to the large fire, watching the shadows jump and warming his bones. Someone passed him a jug and he took a drink of ale, good twice-brewed that went down perfectly. He started to amble away, then turned at the sound of hooves. People riding in along the Newcastle Road.

He stood at the side, a hand raised, hoping they saw him. Three horses, together, slowing to a canter as they reached the houses.

'Welcome, friends,' Josh called loudly. 'What brings you here so late?'

The man in front reined in close, his mount wet with sweat and wild-eyed. The two behind kept their distance, their animals pawing the ground as they breathed heavily.

'I need to speak to the magistrates,' the man said urgently. 'There's important news.'

People had begun to drift over from the fire, curious about the newcomers and pressing closer to see their faces.

'I know him!' someone shouted from the back of the crowd. 'It's that preacher.'

Josh looked up sharply. The horse moved enough for the light to catch the man's face. Aye, it was true enough, Josh thought. That was John Wesley. Two months before they'd been quick enough to pelt him with stones when he stood up to speak. Now they were pressing close to hear whatever news he might be carrying.

'I'll take you,' Josh told him, turning to see Theosophus Johnson and Robert Newman at his side, their cudgels at the ready. 'Gentlemen,' he said to the riders, 'follow me.'

He'd heard some of the aldermen talk about going to the Rose and Crown when they'd gathered to light the bonfire. With luck, a few of them might still be there. It was no more than two hundred yards, the light from the flames bright enough to guide them.

The stable lad came out as soon as he heard voices, taking the beasts as Josh led the men inside. Six of the aldermen were gathered around the table closest to the fire. Some of them looked close to sleep, heads lolling, while three of them laughed and drank. Almost a dozen empty bottles sat between them. Josh coughed, hoping one of them would notice him, then again, louder, when no one turned his head.

'Sirs,' he said in the voice he used to keep order in the town, and waited until the men quieted. Eyes blinked open. 'Mr. Wesley's arrived with important information.'

The preacher stepped forward. He stood tall, looking down with distaste.

'I've just come from the north, sirs. People are fleeing. I've been told that the Pretender's crossed the Tweed. He's in England. You need to prepare, gentlemen.'

There was a brief moment of silence, when time seemed to stand still, then a babble of voices, each one trying to rise above all the others. Josh saw a couple of men slip out. In the room, Alderman Atkinson tried to calm the noise.

He'd heard all he needed. The Scots were south of the border, the Jacobites were coming. He walked out into the night, the fires still burning. But the crowds had gone, simply vanished into the darkness. A few young men wandered, but they looked lost, without purpose.

He marched down Briggate. What would he do if the Scots arrived? Would he take up a sword and fight? Or would he take his wife and his children on the road south, hoping to find safety somewhere.

Suddenly the tune came back into his mind. It was transformed this time, martial and stirring, an accompaniment to his steps. Yes, he thought, this is it. He could already hear the other instruments. It would be excellent for the upcoming balls. If any of them were still here.

Historical Note: In 1745, the Young Pretender – better remembered in history as Bonnie Prince Charlie – was on the move, and all of England was scared. John Wesley, the preacher, had been in Leeds just a few months before, and was pelted with stones and more when he tried to address a crowd. This time, when he returned, it was with the frightening news that the Pretender had crossed the border at Carlisle. It's true that within minutes all the bonfires celebrating November 5th were left, as people took refuge in their houses. At the time, what law and order there was came from the Night Watch, which was made up of the town's musicians, known as the Town Waits, who played for dances and celebrations (and were sometimes engaged to play elsewhere for a fee).

Ballad of a Dead Man – 1749

Tomorrow they'll take me from this place in chains and hang me. From my cell I can see them polishing up the mourning coach that will transport me to the gallows at the Knavesmire. I've already heard them singing the ballads about my death.

The worst part is that it will all happen here in York. I've been a Leeds man all my life and they won't allow me to end it there, the cowards.

But I declare that I, Josiah Fearn, Lord of the Manor of Leeds, am an innocent man. I'll shout it. I'll scream it all the way to the scaffold. I killed Thomas Graves, but everything I did was in self-defence.

Seven hours the trial took. Testimony for and agin. And after that, no more than a few minutes for the jury to reach their verdict. I cried injustice, though no one would listen. So I must write down my account in the hope that it will clear the good name I own.

My father was a clothier. He had no fine start in life, but he was prudent, putting aside the money he made and investing it wisely. When he died he owned properties all over Mabgate and Woodhouse, and two more near the top of Briggate, close by the market cross. I made my home in one of them.

I executed his will, and it was straightforward. Most went to my mother, to be passed in time to my sisters, and a little to myself – one of the houses in Mabgate and the place where I dwelt. For my older brother, Nehemiah? £50 and a paddock in Burmantofts. No more than that, which tells you what my father thought of that wastrel he'd spawned.

I made my living as a drysalter, selling flax and hemp, cochineal and potash, the things people needed. A fair trade it was, but there were those who resented me, who thought I'd come by the little wealth that I possessed too easily. They talked me down behind my back and to my face; they'd raise my ire and challenge me. How can a man back down from that and still think himself a man? There was Joseph Metcalfe for one, who taunted and insulted until I hit him. Then he ran to the night watch, claiming to be in fear of his life. A fine that cost me when it came to court.

I married, to Sarah Dunwell, whose father owned half of Nether Mills, the fulling mill that lies where Sheepscar Beck meets the Aire. He'd worked there a long time, he knew the place in and out. It earned a goodly sum, enough to support the family in handsome style. But old man Dunwell had died, then one of Sarah's sisters and brothers died, so that half the mill should have fallen to my wife. But her mother, the old bitch, refused to give it up, no matter what the law said. The only way she'd agree was if I bought her an estate worth £500. Five hundred pounds! It was enough to give her more than she could hope to spend. Aye, and for her to tell everyone she'd put one over on Josiah Fearn.

But I paid her, and it was worth every penny to be shut of her. Along with Nether Mills came more properties around Quarry Hill and Burmantofts.

We had children, three of them. The first, my boy Josiah, died quick enough, called by the Lord. But then there was John and his sister Sarah. And when my own sister died, all her wealth passed to my John, with me to look after it until he was of age. The Fearns were a family to be reckoned with in Leeds.

The bloody Corporation, the ones who ran Leeds, they had no time for me. They were all merchants, full of fancy clothes and fine words, their noses high in the air. And me, I was no more than the son of clothier, someone who'd come up too far in the world.

'You're an uncouth man, sir,' one of them told me. All because I'd made my money with my own wit and labour and I wasn't afraid to get my hands dirty. I was someone who spoke as I found and that offended those who considered themselves refined. I'd been in court, and my brother, now, had too. We were too rough and ready for the likes of them. But I always knew I'd have my revenge. I'd make sure they remembered my name.

My wife, my lovely Sarah, died in 1731, and my daughter three years later. After that I couldn't bear to live in the house where I'd abided with them and rented it out, moving to a place close to the mill. I bought property cannily, I knew its value. Nether Mills itself was rated at £150 per annum. Only the King's Mill was worth more.

They tried to do me down, the ones who ran things. Twice I was in court for assault, although I'd done nothing. I was fined sixpence on the first occasion, but found not guilty on the second, when a jury wasn't taken in by all the lies. There were other instances when I did what any man should and stood on my pride – those conflicts with my brother Nehemiah, for instance. He'd managed to spend his way through his inheritance and thought I owed him a living. Then there was Benjamin Winn, who believed he could insult my honour with impunity. More fool him.

Then, finally, in 1738, I made sure those on the Corporation couldn't ignore me any more. John Cookson put his share of the manor up for sale and I put my money down and bought it. It was worth every farthing. I owned one-ninth of the manor, and folk had to address me as Lord of the Manor of Leeds. I made sure they bloody well did, too. I'd done my father proud.

Yet still they tried to wear away at me. Where all the other owners of the manor were called Esquire in the minutes, I was plain Mister. No matter. They damned well knew who I was.

I had Tom Grave running Nether Mills for me, just as he did for Mr. Greaves, who owned the other half of the place. Tom lived in the house there, it was part of his pay, and it kept him close in case there was any trouble.

I was an owner who kept up on things. Tom Grave should have reckoned with that. If a ha'penny was spent, I wanted to know where it had gone. He seemed to think he could slip this and that by me, the way he did with Greaves. But I spotted it in the accounts. And as soon as I did, I sacked him from my share and brought in John Crosland, a man I could trust. And I made absolutely sure he had half the house where Grave and his family lived. If Grave had a right to it, so did Crosland.

It all came to a head on Friday, February 24th. I believed Grave was still lining his pockets with money from the mill and I went to the house to confront him. I'd had a little to drink, but what else ought a man do of a night? A flagon or two's never done me any harm.

Grave wasn't there, but his mouse of a wife tried to make me leave, the little shrew. I went, but I wasn't going to be satisfied until I had it out with her husband. An hour later I went back and this time he was there.

He'll have you believe he was meek and mild, leading me out by the hand, importuning me to leave, kind as you please, then helping me up when I fell, insensible from the drink.

Lies! All bloody lies!

He was the one who threw me down on the ground and threatened me. Anyone who's seen him knows he's a brute of a man with the strength of two or three. When he knelt on my chest and threatened to toss me in the mill stream, I believed him. It runs fast and hard, and anyone falling in there is certain to die. He dragged me up by my collar and I feared for my life. He had the glint of murder in his eye. So I did what any man would: I took my knife and stabbed him. And then I went home, to my bed.

They say in court that I was the one who'd threatened him before, but, before the Lord, there's nothing to believe in those accusations.

At two o'clock on the morning of February 25th the night watch came hammering at my door to arrest me and take me before Mayor Scott. I swear the man was smiling as he ordered me to gaol in York Castle.

Tom Grave died on March 2nd. The day before he passed, he gave his statement and damned me in it, may his soul rot. After they held the inquest on him, the charge against me was murder.

The witnesses colluded. They had to do that, so their stories all fit together against mine. And they told them in court, their faces straight in court as they all spouted their tales.

After that, the jury made their verdict and men were selling the broadsheets with the story in the streets.

Aye, the grand men in Leeds will be happy now, and happier still when I'm doing Jack Ketch's dance in the morning at the end of a rope. But they'll not forget the name of Josiah Fearn.

Historical Note: Josiah Fearn should be better known. After all, he was the only Lord of the Manor of Leeds to be executed for murder. At the time it was a sensation and the proceedings of the trial were published. But for all that, it's largely vanished from history, and the man called the 'domineering, villainous Lord of the Manor' vanished. But, as far as we know, it happens as stated here, although the witnesses called in Fearn's defence told a very different, largely unbelievable story. I'm grateful to Margaret Pullen's excellent piece, *Josiah Fearns: A Villainous Lord of the Manor of Leeds*, published in the Second Series, Volume 24 of the Thoresby Society.

Lady Ludd – 1812

'Come and see her,' John said. 'Listen to her.' He hopped around the room on his crutches, twisting and twirling with excitement. 'Come on, Tom. She's worth it, I can promise you that.'

I looked up from my bed. I'd just fallen asleep a few minutes before. It was still light outside, August-bright, but I didn't move. I'd been feeling ill all day. Dog-weary. It had started last night, my stomach lurching, a sweat that broke when I emptied myself, only to come back a few minutes later. In the end I rested a little, no real peace, unable to eat, but drinking down ale like it might cure me. I went to work, down to the wharf. But the only jobs to be had that day were carrying loads from the barges on the Aire. Normally, I'd have been glad of labour like that; it paid better than any other job. Today I just didn't have the strength. I'd have buckled like a spavined horse. Instead I begged for anything to pay a coin or two. Scrubbing decks, coiling the long ropes, tending the horses that pulled the barges. Just enough to pay for the room and ale to slake the thirst that felt like it would consume me. All day my throat was on fire. By the time I finished, all I could do was stumble home and fall on to my bed.

'What do you say?' John asked.

I'd known him since we were little. We'd grown up in the same yard and played together for as long as I could remember. We'd worked jobs together where we could find them. In the mills when we were small, and then whatever came along. Until the recruiting sergeant got him drunk one night in the Fleece and he took the King's Shilling.

They marched him off the next morning and I cursed him roundly for going. Off to Spain with a uniform and a gun to fight Old Boney. Who for? Not for him or me, I knew that much.

A year and he came back, with his right leg rotting in some Spanish field. It had been almost blown off by a Frenchie, and a surgeon had finished the job. They'd brought him back to England, dumped him at the docks in Portsmouth and left him to find his own way home. No pension, no thank you for his service. Not even all the pay the bloody army owed him. Took him a month to find his way back to Leeds.

There was no work for a cripple, of course, nothing but begging for the pennies people could spare, and in these times there were precious few of those. Not with so many scrabbling for anything they could get. The machines, the war; too many out of work. I let him live in my room, a bed of straw and an old sheet in the corner. Not that the place was big enough for two of us, but you can't let a friend down. Between us, we managed to get by. Things would get better. Once this sickness passed, maybe there'd be more loading work.

He'd gone down to the King's Arms last night, on Briggate. That was where he'd heard her. Now he wanted to return for more, and he was pestering me to accompany him, when all I wanted was to lie here and try to sleep a little. Maybe that would help me. If I wasn't at the wharf in the morning I wouldn't earn a farthing.

But he cajoled and persuaded until I couldn't say no. Tired as I felt, dizzy and sweating and holding on to the bricks to keep my step, we were moving slowly towards the inn.

'I'll stand you a cup of ale,' he promised. 'Just stay and listen.'

By the time we arrived the place was already packed. Men and women, all around the walls, every bench filled. The potboy came around and John bought two mugs. I felt sick from the heat, the sweat collecting on my forehead and running down my back. I found a spot with a little air and waited.

They hoisted her up on to a table. She was a slip of a thing in a tattered old gown, small enough to slip into my pocket. But she had a few years on her, hair grey as iron, half her teeth missing, and all the lines of life on her face. She stood there, hands on hips, and looked at us. I could see the fury that burned in her eyes.

'How many of you have gone hungry?' she asked. Daft question. Every one of us had, and she knew it. 'How many have used one of them soup kitchens?'

Every hand was raised. We were all silent, just shuffling a little. I don't know what it was about her, but you had to look, you had to listen; there was no choice. Once she opened her mouth you couldn't take your eyes off her.

'Aye, you know what I mean.' In a bitter winter, the soup was a lifeline when work was scarce and your belly was empty. Free, charity, and I daresay it had saved many in Leeds from dying. 'Some of you had trades before the machines came. You worked with your hands and you could provide for your families. They didn't go hungry and you had a roof over your head. Then good Mr. Gott brought in his gig mills that take away jobs. All the more brass for him in his big house in Armley and less for the likes of us. Or what about Shann's selling cloth that had little honest labour in it?

The owners will take your jobs away and tell you it's progress. They'll see you starve for all they care.' She surveyed the crowd. 'All that matters to them is how much precious money they have. You know what I say?'

'What?' someone shouted from the other side of the room.

'I say damn them and their purses. It's time ordinary folk didn't have to starve.'

There was a cheer at that, but she waved them down with her hands.

'The only way we're going to do that is to take what's ours.' The cheering stopped with those words. 'Let them see that we won't be cowed.'

'And how are going to do that, luv?' another voice asked.

'We're going to go out on the street tomorrow – all of us – and we're taking it.' She waited through a buzz of muttering. 'It's market day, there'll be plenty of folk about. You know how they're scared of a mob, so we'll give them a mob to frighten them.' She cackled, and her eyes moved slowly over every face. 'Who's with me?'

They yelled and roared. But they would, folk were desperate. Too many went to bed with their bellies empty at night. Too many had nowhere to sleep at all. It had been bad times since the machines and the war started. Too long. They made us slave for the scraps from a rich man's table and told us we should be grateful to get them. And all the while the clergy told us we'd find our reward in heaven. Old Ned Ludd and his gang had done well, he'd scared those with money. But it wasn't enough. Nothing would ever really be enough.

I shouted with the rest of them and so did John. But I knew I wouldn't be there. If I was well enough in the morning I'd go down to the wharf and hope for some work. If not, I'd be in my bed. I felt hotter than ever, overcome by everything around me, as if I might pass out. I held the mug against my face. It helped, but only a little.

'What's your name, lass?' a voice called.

She brought a fan from her sleeve, opened it and fluttered the thing in front of her face, her eyes hard and brilliant as jewels.

'You can call me Lady Ludd,' she answered after a moment, and everyone laughed. 'Be here in the morning. All of you.' And when she said it, I believed she was looking at me.

'I was right, wasn't I?' John said as we went slowly home. For once I was glad there was no speed in his walk, just the constant effort of his crutches.

'Maybe.' They were words. Good words, yes, but what did those ever achieve? The air was still warm, but it felt good and fresh after being cooped up with so many folk.

'Are you going to come tomorrow?'

'Maybe,' I repeated.

John was ready early, eager for us to be on our way.

'I can't,' I told him. 'I feel so poorly.'

I'd been up three times during the night, filling the bowl. The room stank, I knew that and it shamed me, but I hadn't had the strength to open the window and throw the slops out. I lay there sweating, feeling like my stomach had turned to hot liquid.

'I'll bring something back for you,' he said.

He didn't, and maybe just as well. I couldn't have eaten anything. By the time he returned I'd slept a little. But pain had started to rack me, leaving me twisting and turning, trying to find a way, any way at all, to lie comfortably.

I heard his crutches on the stair as he eased himself up, a bang and a pause with each step. I knew it took a lot from him. But this room in the attic was better than living on the street. Finally the door opened and he came in, face red from the strain, the way it always was.

'You should have been there, John,' he told me, and I nodded. 'A hundred of us if there was one.' With a grunt, he settled on to his pallet. 'All of us going round the market. Lady Ludd kept yelling out to the farmers and the corn dealers, telling them how we were starving here and they should show some Christian feeling. Then someone tried to knock down one of our lads and ended up with four of them on him for his trouble. And all the while she was taunting and yelling. Fights everywhere for a while. People were kicking over the stalls. Then one of ours smashed one of the shop windows and someone ran off for the militia.' His eyes were shining with the joy of battle. All I could do was lie there and listen. I didn't have the will to move. 'A man from the soup kitchen came out and said they had dried fish for sale. Threepence a pound.'

It was a good price. Fair if you had threepence. I knew many who didn't. But it would feed a family.

'What happened?' My voice was hardly more than a croak. John lifted my head and poured some ale into my mouth. I could feel it draining straight through me.

'Half of them left to buy it. That Lady Ludd stood up there

and talked, trying to convince the people at the market that they should be with us. You ought to have heard it. People were screaming and shouting. Then a lad ran up and passed the word that the militia were coming.' He grinned happily. 'You've never seen a crowd disappear so fast. Took everything they could carry, and damn the farmers and the bakers.'

I could understand. When you're starving, a loaf looked like gold and a chicken could be the taste of heaven.

'How do you feel now, Tom?' he asked, gently tipping a little more ale into my mouth. I swallowed, for all the good it would do. I reached out with my hand and took hold of his arm. His skin felt so cool.

'Help me, John. Please. I think I'm dying.'

Historical Note: The Luddites have been praised and damned. They started out in Nottinghamshire in 1811, supposedly under the command of 'General' Ned Ludd, breaking the machines that were taking away jobs. But that was nothing new around Leeds; there'd been incidents of machine-breaking in 1797 in both Hunslet and Beeston. The riot led by Lady Ludd climaxed a dangerous few months in 1812. Fires had been set, and in August the King's Mill on Swinegate was attacked just before the Briggate Riot. By November several detachments of troops had been sent in to try and avert more trouble from the starving population.

Waterloo Lake – 1815

The foreman looked at him doubtfully.

'I don't know, lad. This is a job that needs muscle. You've not got much of that.'

Joe breathed deeply. How many times had he gone through this in the last six months?

'I've been all over England looking for work, sir. I can do my share and more. If I don't, just turn me out. But there's not much food on the road.'

Not much in his belly, either, he thought. Berries that he'd found that morning on his way here, the charity of his sister's bench for sleeping and a loaf of bread in Leeds yesterday.

'You were in the army, you said?' The foreman had a grizzled face and wide, scarred knuckles. His breeches were thick and patched, old boots scuffed to nothing.

'Yes, sir. The Fourteenth. Started in the first battalion and then in the second as a corporal.'

'The peninsula?'

'Yes, sir. Spain and we followed Wellington up into France. And served in the Lowlands, too, when we were there.' Joe turned his head and spat at the memory. Half his platoon had died of Walcheren fever and they'd never fired a shot.

The foreman chewed at a fingernail as he thought.

'From Leeds?' he asked.

'Long time ago,' Joe admitted. After twelve years away fighting it didn't feel like home. But nowhere did. He'd only drifted back because he'd run out of other places to go. And then he'd found that his mam and the bastard she'd married were both dead, his brothers scattered who knew where. Only Emily left, and that husband of hers had been grudging enough about a night's lodging. At least he'd told him about the work here. A landowner making a lake he'd said, and employing men who'd been in the army. Happen they'd take you on, he said.

'I'll give you a chance,' the foreman decided finally. 'Tuppence a day and two quarts of beer. But if you don't pull your weight, you'll be gone. He pointed to a hut in the distance. 'Report over there.'

'Yes, sir.' He hesitated a moment, then asked, 'Is it right that this is going to be a lake?'

'Aye. Mr. Nicholson thinks it'll look better like that. More harmonious, he said.' He scratched his head and looked at the long deep scar in the ground that stretched for a good half mile. 'Can't say as he's wrong, neither. Better than a bloody quarry, any road.' The creases on the foreman's face turned into a smile. 'Going to name it Waterloo Lake, celebrate the victory. Were you there, lad?'

Joe shook his head. The army had paid him off after they'd caught Boney for the first time. Cast him adrift in England without even a thank you for the thousands of miles he'd marched, all the powder and shot he'd fired or the friends left on battlefields. There'd been hundreds like him, thousands maybe. They could spot each other with ease, skin darkened by years of foreign sun and the eyes of men who'd thought they were needed only to discover that they weren't once the cannon stopped roaring.

He was better off than some; he still had all his limbs and his wits. He could work. He would have, too, if there'd been any jobs. He'd worked where he could, begged when he had to. He'd been moved on from parishes by beadles, sentenced to seven days in jail as a vagrant down South when all he wanted was to earn his keep. Tuppence was a fair wage. It was only September. The days were still hot, the nights warm and dry enough to sleep outside. He'd be able to find somewhere around here. God knew, there was enough space.

He marched across to the hut, aware that people would be watching him, judging him. The door was open, a man studying a drawing weighted down on a table. A gentleman, from the cut of his clothes. Joe stood at attention for a minute, waiting for him to turn, then gave a small cough. The man looked up quickly, blinking against the sunlight.

'You must be a new man.'

'Yes, sir. Joseph Colton, sir.'

'Old John decided you were worth a try, did he?' The man had a calm smile and an easy manner.

'Yes, sir. I suppose so, sir.' He'd say whatever the man wanted. Tuppence a day would see him right for a while.

'Do you have any engineering training, Mr. Colton?'

'No, sir. Just building ramparts in Spain, that's all.'

'Good.' The man's smile widened. 'That's more or less what we're doing here. We're making a dam to create a lake.' He came out, ducking his head under the low lintel. 'You see over there, that low side? We're digging out from the bottom to dam it all there. There's another lake. We're going to bring in water from there and it'll look perfect.'

'Yes, sir.' Joe gazed around. There had to be fifty or sixty men in the quarry, some digging, others moving earth in carts, by hand or goading donkeys along. 'Is that what I'll be doing, sir?'

'It is, Mr. Colton. We need the dam finished before winter comes.' The man raised his eyes. 'Mind you, that might be a while yet if God keeps smiling on us like this. You were a soldier?'

'In the Fourteenth.'

'Ah, good!' The man beamed, the sun catching his fair hair so it almost seemed white. 'The West Yorkshires as was. Right. There's a path cut just over there. Mattocks and spades are at the bottom. And the ale barrel, of course,' he added quickly. 'Start at six, dinner at eleven, finish at six.' He drew a watch on a fine gold chain from the pocket of his waistcoat and pursed his lips thoughtfully. 'It's just gone eight. You work hard and I think we can stretch to paying you for a full day.'

'Thank you, sir.'

Calling it a path was generous, Joe decided. In places some of the dirt had crumbled away so that the track was less than a foot wide, and a sheer drop into the quarry for anyone who fell. He walked carefully, testing each pace forward, until he reached the bottom.

By six the worst of the heat had faded from the day. He sat in the welcome shade of a tree, sipping from a mug of ale. Simply walking back up from the bottom had seemed like an impossible effort. He'd spent the day shovelling earth onto an endless procession of carts. By dinner he felt as if there was a fire in his back and his shoulders. He'd forced himself to continue through the afternoon, the sun on him. Blisters grew and burst on his hands, then more came until he could barely take hold of anything.

When work was done he'd waited for the foreman to return and pocketed his wages.

'You can come back tomorrow,' the man told him. 'You're hired on.'

He still had half the loaf his sister had given him and a blanket in his pack. All he needed was somewhere by a stream and he'd be fine for the night. A group of workers passed, raising their arms in a weary salute.

'Where are you staying?' one of them called and Joe only shrugged. He wanted a little longer here first, settled under the coolness of an oak.

'We've got a camp,' another said. 'You might as well come

and join us.'

Slowly, Joe pushed himself upright. It was like Spain, when every rest only made going on more difficult. You continued because you had to, because not moving meant a whipping or death from the robbers who roamed the country.

He caught up with them close to the top of the lake, where woods came down to the water.

'We're over there. Plenty of room.' The man gave a hoarse laugh. 'Did you I hear you say earlier that you were from Leeds?'

'Aye,' Joe agreed. 'Once.'

'Changed much?'

'I suppose so.' More people, the chimneys of the manufactories with their smoke, the streets full and feeling dangerous. Or perhaps he'd been the one to change.

'Welcome home, anyway,' the man said.

Historical Note: Thomas Nicholson bought the area that's now Roundhay Park in 1803. He improved it greatly, building a home – now the Mansion – and constructing Waterloo Lake where a quarry had stood (he also had the Upper Lake built to disguise scars on the landscape). He used men who'd returned from the Napoleonic Wars for the job, people who'd come home to find there were no jobs. It was, if you like, an early social enterprise scheme. They constructed a dam at the side of the lake that leads out towards Wetherby Road. John Barran, then Mayor of Leeds, purchased the park in 1871, and after an Act of Parliament, Leeds bought it from him. Prince Arthur opened the park the following year, although it didn't become popular for another two decades, until electric trams had a terminus there, giving easy access.

The Factory Lad's Testimony – 1836

He came in, walking slowly, almost in a shuffle, using a stick to keep himself balanced. His knees bent inward, making each step awkward. Still holding the doorknob he peered around the room, straining his eyes the way a mole might. He wore thick spectacles, almost a frail old man, although he couldn't have been more than twenty.

The three members of the factory commission – Mr, Turnbull, Mr. Wakefield, and Sir Edward Jepson - sat behind their table as a clerk put papers in front of them. There was an air of sleekness about them; they all looked comfortable with authority.

The young man was wearing his best clothes, a dark jacket, cut high at the waist, a stock and shirt, with breeches and thick woollen hose. On the other side of the room a fire burned in the grate.

'Come in, please, sir, and sit yourself down,' Sir Edward said. 'Thank you for coming to speak to us.'

The young man bowed his head slowly and crossed the floor, his heels tapping on the boards. He sat as upright as any defendant, his back straight, eyes squinting to take in the faces: the commissioners, the pair of clerks and the scribe waiting with his paper and steel nib to take down every word.

'What's your name and what do you do?' Mr. Wakefield asked.

'Sir, my name is John Dawson,' the young man began, repeating the words when he was asked to speak more loudly, 'and I make my living as a tailor when I'm well enough to work.' He glanced at his audience. 'As you can see, sir, that my eyesight is bad. That's why I wear these glasses.'

'Do you believe there's a reason for your bad eyesight?' Mr Turnbull wondered.

'I do, sir,' Dawson answered with a nod. 'If you ask me, it's from the flax mills I worked in as a lad. There's always a powerful lot of dust in the air and it does affect the eyes of some folk. I daresay as I'd be blind now if I still worked there.'

'When did you begin in the mills?'

'I started in the mills when I was six, sir, a doffer at Shaw and Tennant's. The work wasn't too hard, we had to take the full bobbins off the machines and put on empty ones. But the hours were long, six in the morning to seven at night, six days a week. I was lucky, my da was the overlooker in the room. He beat me, same way he beat the other doffers, but not too bad, not as hard as some,' he added, as if it was the most natural thing in the world. 'It was the standing all the time that was worst. Every day my knees ached.'

'Did you receive any education?' Sir Edward asked.

'Not as you'd call it, sir.' Dawson held his head up to face his audience. 'I always wanted to learn to read and write. And I went to Sunday school whenever I could, unless my ma needed me to be with the younger bairns or I had no decent clothes or shoes. My da taught me to read, and I was middling good with the Testament.'

'But that was all?'

'It was, sir.'

'Please continue,' Mr. Wakefield told him, with a glance at the others.

'My da left Tennant's when I was ten, and I went with him to Garside's Mill.'

'Do you know why he left?'

'I do not, sir, no. I was just a boy, so they never told me. At Garside's they put me to work bobbin-hugging, and that was terrible hard work, sir. I had to carry around a basket full of bobbins, some of them still wet. The basket was on my back, and big it was, held in place by a strap around my forehead.' He moved his hands to illustrate, each of the commissioners nodding. 'I often had to carry full baskets up the stairs to the reelers. My knees were so bad that I had to stop after two or three years. You could see them, all bent, but we had no money for a doctor.'

'No one looked after you there at all?'

'No sir. They worked us hard there. After a while my da and I left. We went to Clayton's, and I was made a doffer again.'

'Did that help you at all? Mr. Turnbull said.

'The work was easier but the hours were bad. Sometimes five in the morning to half-past nine at night. They gave us forty minutes for us dinner but nothing for breakfast or drinking.' The lad's voice was quite even, not angry. Just remembering his life of a few years before. 'Wasn't always six days we worked. Sometimes there was only enough for five or four. Weeks like that didn't bring home enough money.' He removed his spectacles and polished them on a piece of linen he took from the pocket of his waistcoat. When he spoke he was quieter. 'It was dangerous work there, too. I knew one lad whose clothes caught in an upright shaft and he was killed, and there were other bad accidents I can recall, too. My da died after

I'd been there a few years, and when my ma was taken ill we had to go into the workhouse. By then my knees were bent so bad I couldn't walk more than thirty yards without a rest.'

'Might we see your knees, Mr.' – Sir Edward stared down at the page – '-Mr. Dawson. If you'd be so good.'

Holding on to the chair with one hand, Dawson stood and unbuckled the knees of his breeches, rolling them up. His face was red, not from effort but the embarrassment of being watched so closely.

It was just as he'd said. His knees were misshapen things, bent forward and inwards into something grotesque, beyond human.

'Thank you,' Sir Edward told him quickly, looking away and conferring with the other commissioners while Dawson closed his breeches buttons and sat once more.

'You said you went to the workhouse,' Mr. Turnbull continued.

'That's right, sir.' Dawson gave a quick nod of his head.

'What was your experience there?'

'It was good, sir. At the workhouse they taught me my trade, sir, made a tailor out of me. It's better than I might have had otherwise. And I did see someone about my knees. They sent me to Mr. Chorley at the infirmary.'

'Was he able to help you at all?'

'Very much, sir.' There was heartfelt gratitude in Dawson's voice. 'He gave me strengthening plasters and bandages and they did me some good. You can see it's still difficult for me to walk, sir, and I need a stick to help me. But it's better than it was, and I'm very grateful for that. It used to be I couldn't manage thirty yards without a rest. Now I can walk a hundred yards and more before I need to stop.' He gave a proud smile.

Sir Edward looked over at the other commissioners. Many more waiting outside to be interviewed before the day was done. Surgeons, overseers, workers, people from all walks of life. When Turnbull and Wakefield shook their heads, he turned back to Dawson.

'Sir, thank you for coming here today. You've been most gracious with your time and we wish you well as a tailor.'

They waited silently as John Dawson left the room, leaning heavily on his stick.

Historical Note: The Factory Commissioners toured England in 1833, gathering evidence to report on the employment of children.

They interviewed a number of people in Leeds, including John Dawson. All I've done is paraphrase his words.

Jenny White – 1850

Jenny White was a pretty lass; everyone told her that.

'That face is your fortune,' her mam said when she was young. Said it so often that Jenny believed her. And from the time she was old enough, all the lads courted her. They'd bring her things – a few flowers picked on a lane, something shiny found by the river – and she'd reward them with a kiss.

She was a mill hand, long hours from early until late, dust in the air to clog the lungs, all the smoke and soot from the chimneys in the streets. But when work was done and she'd been home for her supper, Jenny was ready to have some fun. Dancing to the fiddlers, singing the songs she'd always known. Laughing. Life might be hard, but there was room for fun in it, too.

While the young men threw their caps at her and she'd kiss their cheeks, she only had eyes for Joshua. From the very first time she saw him, she knew. He was a handsome fellow, with dark hair and cruel eyes. He was a clerk at the mill, with a good, clear hand and a quick mind. Whenever she could, Jenny would go to the office, hoping he'd notice her, that he'd strike up a conversation. But he paid her no mind. Why would he? With his looks, an easy smile and a flattering tongue, he could have any girl he wanted.

But the other clerks noticed Jenny. Every time she'd been in the office, with her hopeful look, they'd tease him.

'She's sweet on you, lad.'

'If you don't want her, I'll take her.'

He laughed with them. But finally, one day when she brought some papers to his desk, he looked at her properly. Pretty enough, he agreed. The type who'd make a good wife, do as she was told.

They began to keep company. A walk by the river when the evening was warm. Dancing. She was willing. Whatever he suggested, she wanted to do it. Where boys usually did her bidding, for Josh she'd make all the time she had. She loved him with all her heart.

That was her weakness; he saw it and he used it. He'd promise to meet her then never arrive, leaving her waiting for hours, lonely and crying. And even when they were together, his attention would be fleeting, easily taken elsewhere. A game of dice, a shapely leg could distract him. It was only when they were alone that she felt he was really with her, and in those moments she was happy.

She could win him completely, Jenny felt sure. Whenever she was going to be with him she took special care over her appearance. Some ribbon in her hair. A dress she'd sewn, working by candelight until she could barely make out the stitches any more.

When Joshua suggested they should wed, at first she couldn't believe it. It was what she wanted – *all* she'd wanted since she saw him – but he'd never shown a sign of it before. The joy poured through her, gushing out when she told her mam and dad. They looked at each other doubtfully.

'I'd not do it,' her father advised, sitting by the hearth and puffing on his clay pipe. 'There's no good in that young man.'

'But he asked me to marry him,' Jenny said. 'He must love me.'

'Men do funny things, luv,' her mother said. 'Think twice. Allus think twice.'

She didn't need to; this was what she desired.

It was a small wedding, the vows quickly exchanged, the celebration in a public house with the groom and his friends drinking until the landlord called time on them. A quick fumble in the bed, enough to claim her maidenhead, and he was asleep, waking with a sore head and a foul temper she'd never seen before.

He might not be perfect, she told herself, but at least he was hers forever. She could learn what he wanted, make sure she pleased him. And he'd change. When he realised how much he meant to her, he was bound to feel more tender towards her.

But Jenny soon learned that married life with Joshua Green was worse than courting him. Much worse. He'd stay out in the public houses until all hours, coming home drunk and taking his anger out on her. A smack at first that startled her and made her cry. He seemed to enjoy her pain. Some nights he used his belt on her, others he'd take her by the hair and pull her around the room. She learned not to yell or scream; that only seemed to excite him more.

He was careful. He only bruised her where it wouldn't show. She couldn't go and tell her mam and dad. She was too proud to admit she'd been wrong, that she'd made her mistake with Joshua and put herself in hell. Then it was too late. The winter took both her parents, within days of each other, when pneumonia came and there was nothing anyone could do to save them.

With one sister in Wakefield, married and with three children of her own, the other gone to Bradford to do God only knew what, Jenny was on her own.

She came to dread the nights, lying in bed, unable to sleep, simply waiting for his footsteps and what new pleasure he'd concocted. The only time he smiled was when he was hurting her, as if it made him stronger. Once he choked her until she passed out, hoping he'd kill her and put an end to it. When she came to he was watching her and laughing softly.

She knew her letters from Sunday school. Now, when she could find a scrap of paper, she tried to put down what she felt. Jenny scratched with the nib, attempting to put all her pain into words.

The marriage vows as false as dicers' oaths. The road with no fork until the grave. Tears like gall.

And then one night Joshua didn't come home. The sun rose, she went off to her job at the mill, dazed, wondering. Had something happened to him? Was he dead? Please God, she thought, let him be dead and judged for all he's done.

But under it all, the fear, the hatred, she knew she still loved him. That was her curse, to still want him the way she had when she first saw him. She'd tried to banish the feelings, but she couldn't make them leave. They dragged at her heart.

She worked the day in a daze, berated three times by the foreman, blushing each time he told her off. Her wages would be docked, she knew, but she didn't care. Later she went from pub to pub until she found where Josh had been the night before and the landlord told her he'd left at closing, a young lass on his arm.

He didn't come back that night, nor the one after it, or ever again. She asked all over Leeds, seeking word of him until someone said Josh had gone to Halifax with his lass and she broke down in tears.

She should have been happy. It was over, he wouldn't ever hurt her again. But the news made her feel as if she was on the lip of a deep pit, staring down and unable to see the bottom. She'd done everything he wanted. He'd taken it all, and it hadn't been enough. He'd still wanted someone else.

Jenny began to walk. He'd broken her body and now he'd broken her heart. She knew which was worse. Her stomach felt empty, like something was gnawing away at it, but she still wanted to be sick.

She wandered. She didn't know how long, she didn't pay any attention to where she went. All hither and yon. She was lost inside her mind. Thoughts tumbled. Memories flitted through, pictures that slid away, one following another.

Jenny came to a gap between the houses. Cold air on her

face. She breathed in the stink of the river, dead and dank. In front of her, steps led down to the water. Without thinking, as if she was trapped in a dream, Jenny followed them, stair by stair, one foot in front of the other. As she did, her spirits began to lighten. She might fly away, be gone from this place. Down she went, and the water of the river lapped around her feet. Down further until it reached her knees.

She never even heard the shout. The water was carrying her. Not as cold as it seemed, it lulled and buoyed her. Jenny's head went under and she smiled.

People ran when they heard yelling. Someone took a boat out on the water, with an oil lamp to search. But there was no Jenny in the river. She'd moved out of sight and out of this world. No body was ever found, although people searched for days, all the way down to Knostrop.

Some said she must have drowned. Others wanted to believe she'd drifted until she found a place where lovers spoke truly. Where hearts were safe and words were bonds. Perhaps she'd slipped through to somewhere she could smile and laugh again. But it seemed as if Jenny White had gone through a hole in the world.

Historical Note: On The Calls, there was a set of stairs that went down to the River Aire. It was set in a gap between two buildings and known as Jenny White's Hole, named for the woman who supposedly drowned there after discovering that her love was untrue to her. No body ever seems to have been found, but fragments of Jenny's writings were later discovered.

Annabelle Atkinson and Mr. Grimshaw – 1879

Inspired by the painting *Reflections on the Aire: On Strike, Leeds 1879*, by Atkinson Grimshaw

On both sides of the river, rows of factory chimneys stood straight and tall and silent, bricks blackened to the colour of night. Smoke was only rising from a few today, but the smell of soot was everywhere, on the breath and on the clothes. It was the shank of an October afternoon and the gas lamps were already lit, dusk gathering in the shadows.

He stood and looked at the water. Where barges should be crowded against the warehouses like puppies around a teat there was nothing. Just a single boat moored in the middle of the Aire, no sails set, its masts spindly and bare as a prison hulk.

He coughed a little, took the handkerchief from his pocket and spat delicately into it. This was the time of year when it always began, when men and women found their lungs tender, when the foul air caught and clemmed in the chest and the odour from the gasworks cut through everything so that even the bitter winter snow tasted of it.

What sun there was hung low in the west, half-hidden by clouds. A few more minutes and he'd be finished, then walk home to Knostrop, leaving the stink and stench of Leeds for trees and grass and the sweet smell of fresher air. First, though, he needed to complete the sketch, to capture these moments.

Tomorrow he'd start in the studio, to try and find the mood that overwhelmed him now, Leeds in the still of the warehousemen's strike, no lading, no voices shouting, no press of people and trade along the river.

'What tha' doing?'

He turned. He hadn't heard her come along the towpath. But there she was, peering over his shoulder at the lines on the pad, the shadings and simple strokes that were his shorthand.

'Tha' drawing?'

'Sketching,' he answered with a smile and slipping the charcoal into his jacket pocket.

'Aye, it's not bad,' she told him with approval, reaching out a finger with the nail bitten short and rimmed with dirt. 'I like that,' she said, pointing at the way he'd highlighted the buildings as they vanished towards the bridge, hinting at the cuts and alleys and what lay beyond.

'Thank you.'

He studied her properly, a girl who was almost a woman, in an old dress whose pattern had faded, the hem damp and discoloured where she'd walked across the wet grass. She wore her small, tattered hat pinned into her hair.

At most she was twenty, he judged. As she opened her mouth to speak he could see that one of her teeth was missing, the others yellowed, and her face held the start of lines that belonged to a woman twice her age. Her cheeks were sunk from hunger, the bones of her wrists like twigs. But her eyes were clear and full of mischief. She carried a bundle in her left hand. At first he thought she was a ragpicker, done for the day; then he noticed how she cradled it close and understood it was what little she owned in the world.

'What's your name?' he asked.

'Anabelle Atkinson, sir,' she replied with the faintest of smiles. 'Me mam said she wanted summat nice around her.'

He nodded, watching the water and the sky again. In a minute the clouds would part, leaving the sun pale as lemon reflecting on the river. Perhaps the last sun of the year, except for a few days when it would sparkle on the snow around his home. He held his breath for a moment, ready to work quickly.

'My name's Atkinson, too,' he said distracted by the light, committing it to memory.

'Happen as we're related, then.' He could feel her eyes on him. 'But mebbe not.'

'It's my middle name,' he explained quietly, 'but I prefer it to my Christian name.'

'Why's that, then?'

Very quickly he fumbled in his pocket, drawing out coloured pencils and adding to the sketch, the reflections on the river, the gold of a fading sun mingling with the browns and greens of the dirty water, smudging with the edge of his hand, thinking, putting it all away in his memory for tomorrow when he'd sit in the studio with his paints.

'It suits me better,' he answered her finally, squinting at his work, then at the scene before adding some more touches.

'That's right,' she said slowly, as he was about to add more umber to the water. 'That's it.' There was awe in her voice, as if she couldn't believe nature could be captured that way. 'It looks alive.'

'It's just preparation,' he explained. 'I'll paint it soon.'

'That what you are, then? An artist?'

'I am.'

He was a successful one, too. Whatever he put on canvas sold, almost before it had dried. For the last nineteen years it had been his living, since he broke away from the tedium of working as a railway clerk, the job he thought might crush his heart. With no training and only the support of his wife, he'd known that painting could make his soul sing. These days he was a wealthy man, one who'd made art pay him well. Now they knew him all around the country; in London any man would deign to receive him.

'You must make a bob or two.'

Grimshaw smiled.

'I get by.'

'You've got good clothes and you talk posh.'

He chuckled.

'Don't be fooled. I'm not as posh as you'd think. I grew up in Wortley and my father worked on the railways. What about you, Annabelle Atkinson? Where do you live?'

'Me mam's in one of them houses up on the Bank.'

He knew them, squalid back-to-backs with no grass or green, some of the worst housing in Leeds. No good air and the children ragged as tinkers' brats. It was where the Irish lived, crammed together in dwellings that everyone said should be pulled down.

'How many of you?'

'Only four now. I'm not there no more, though. Had a job as a maid in one of them big houses out past Headingley.'

'Had?' He eyed her sharply.

'They didn't like me having gentleman callers. Said it wasn't proper for someone in my station.' She put on a voice as she spoke and her eyes flashed with anger. 'Me mam won't have me back. No room, not if I'm not bringing in a wage.'

'What are you going to do?'

She shrugged.

'I'll find summat. There's always work for them as is willing to graft.'

He thought of the life in her and of his own children, six alive and the ten who'd died. And of his wife, twenty-two years married, with her stern face and the eternal look of weariness.

'Where are you going to sleep?'

'There's rooms. At least when they turned me out they paid what they owed. I'll not go short for a while.'

He looked down at the sketch. It caught everything well, and it would be a good painting, another one to bring in a good ten pounds or more. But it was a landscape unpeopled.

'Annabelle Atkinson, can you do something for me?'

'What?' she asked warily, too familiar with the ways of men.

'Just stand about ten yards down the path, that's all.'

'Why?'

He tapped the drawing with a fingernail.

'I want to put you in this, that's all?'

'Me?' She laughed. 'Go on, you don't want me in that.'

'I do. Please.'

She shook her head, smiling all the while.

'You're daft, you are.' But she still moved along the path, looking back over her shoulder. 'Here?'

'Yes. Look out over the river. That's it. Stay there.'

He was deft, seeing how she held the bundle, her bare arms, the hem of the dress high enough to show bare ankles, and a sense of longing in the way she held herself.

'I'm done,' he told her after a minute and she came back to him.

'That's me?' she asked.

'It is.'

'Do I really look like that?'

'That's how I see you,' he said with a smile. She kept staring at the paper.

'You'll put that in your painting?'

'With more detail, yes.'

'What?'

'The pattern of the dress, things like that.'

Self-consciously she smoothed down the old material, her face suddenly proud, looking younger and less careworn. He dug into his trouser pocket, pulling out two guineas.

'This is for you.'

'What? All this?'

'I'm an artist. I pay my models.'

'But I didn't do owt. I just stood over there,' she protested.

'I sketched you, and you'll be in the painting. That makes you my model. Here, take it.'

Almost guiltily she plucked the money from his hand, tucking it away in the pocket of her dress.

'Thank you, sir,' she said quietly. 'You've made my day,

you have.'

'As you've made mine, Annabelle Atkinson.' He closed the sketch pad and put away the pencils and charcoal, then tipped his hat to her before walking away.

'So what is your name, then?' she asked.

'Atkinson Grimshaw.' He handed her his card. 'I wish you and your baby well.'

'Me in a painting. There's no one as'll believe that.' She began to laugh, letting it rise into a full-throated roar, and he laughed with her.

Historical Note: Leeds has associations with one or two great artists. In the late 19th century Atkinson Grimshaw achieved both acclaim and commercial success, a rare combination. He had the beautiful ability to paint moonlight and his evening Leeds scenes are well-known. But there's another painting of the Aire, painted during a strike in 1879, no traffic on the water, few people around, that possesses something very special. For me it has an extra dimension – this is the story that brought me Annabelle, or an early version of her, to reappear in a few other stories and the Tom Harper series of crime novels.

Wonderland – 1884

They chose us careful enough. Interviewed by a matron and by the manager, Mr. Monteith himself. Not just questions, but our elocution and deportment, as well as our behaviour. Mr. Monteith explained that he had a standard he expected at such a place as Monteith, Hamilton and Monteith, and the matron, Miss Hardisty, nodded her agreement.

The customer, he said, must feel like royalty. His girls would be well turned-out. Anyone who wasn't would be sent home without pay, and if it happened twice, that would be the end of her employment.

He was a very neat man, Mr. Monteith. Precise in his speech and his dress. He wore a proper frock coat. You don't see that too often any more. His teeth and his fingernails were clean, and his hair had a light sheen of pomade. At first I thought he looked more like a mannequin than a man. But once he began talking about this department store, you could see the passion in his eyes. Perhaps it was strange to become so excited about a thing like that, but that's how he was.

I knew how to behave. I'd spent seven years in service, since I was nine years old, and I had excellent references to prove it. Scullery maid, upstairs maid, then a ladies' maid, I'd done it all. Good teachers I'd had, too. This shop work would be easier. It would pay better and I'd be in my own bed every night, instead of going back to visit my parents one afternoon a week.

Mr. Monteith read each reference carefully, nodding his head at a phrase here, a word there. He passed them to Miss Hardisty. She glanced at them quickly then sat, smiling.

Finally he raised his head. He'd made a decision.

'Miss Allison, your Christian name is Victoria, is that correct?'

Yes sir. I was named for the Queen.'

'Well, Miss Allison, I'd be gratified to offer you a position with us at the terms I outlined to you at the beginning of this interview. You seem to be an ideal candidate.' His face was serious, eyes intent upon me. 'Do you wish to join us?'

'Yes sir, I do.' I was beaming and trying to sound calm, but inside I wanted to shout for joy. Working in a place like this? It would be like coming to some magic land every day.

'Excellent.' He gave a quick smile, as if he was unused to

the gesture. 'Miss Hardisty will show you the department store, assign you your duties and see that you receive your uniform.'

'Thank you, sir.' I offered him a small curtsey, not quite sure what to do.

'You've had experience as a ladies' maid. I think perhaps a position in the ladies' wear department, don't you?' He looked vaguely at Miss Hardisty.

'Absolutely,' she agreed quickly. 'Come along, Miss Allison. You need to learn where everything is.'

She walked away briskly and I hurried to follow. She wore a cotton dress, no bustle, walking with her spine very straight and shoulders back, hair gathered in a tight bun on the top of her head.

'We shall have two hundred staff by the time we open,' she told me. 'Young ladies *and* young gentlemen. I trust I don't need to say that we shall frown upon any fraternisation.'

'Of course, miss,' I agreed. But I knew the rule was unlikely to work, and was glad about it.

Men in brown coats or heavy aprons were setting out the goods according to a plan. Monteith's covered four floors in a new building that still smelt of distemper. On the top floor, workmen were laying the carpet and we had to walk gingerly around them, trying to ignore their comments.

The department store was larger than any building I'd been in before. Girls I knew talked about the size of Temple Mill, but I didn't see how it could compare to this.

'You will be working on the second floor, Miss Allison. As Mr. Monteith said, we expect the highest standards for our staff. Politeness to the customers at all times and very prompt service. It will be our hallmark.'

It took more than an hour to explore the whole place. Four floors. Four! I felt sure I'd be lost every day when I made my way around. Not only was there the area open to the public, but also behind the doors, where we kept our stock, and a cafeteria for staff in the basement, along with lockers where we might keep our valuables.

Outside, in the spring air, I looked around. I followed the tall plate glass windows around on to Boar Lane. I was going to be working here. I wanted to sing, to laugh. But I knew I had to act with decorum now.

I began work the next Monday. Still a week to go before the opening, and we were bustling round, preparing everything. Young men were working in the windows to create the displays. The inside of the glass had been covered with newspaper so that people outside couldn't see. It was a smart idea, I thought. It created a sense of anticipation. On the second floor we were arranging the clothing, making everything tempting and just so.

Each morning I was proud to change into my uniform and present myself for inspection to the floor supervisor, Miss Adams. She was as demanding as any sergeant-major, looking at our nails and the shine on our shoes, as well as the arrangement of our hair and the cleanliness of our clothes.

'She's a right madam,' Catherine said to me as we set out blouses on one of the counters. We'd been assigned to work together, and for the first day I'd been unsure. Catherine was a few years older than me, and worldly in a way I wasn't. She'd been in a mill, she'd been in service, and she'd worked in a milliner's shop before. She understood life.

'Is she?' I asked. When I worked for the family in Chapel Allerton we'd had the same kind of inspection each day.

'Course she is. Look at her, she's like a dried up prune. Probably never had a night's fun in her life.' She winked. 'You know what I mean?'

I stifled a giggle.

'You know what people are calling this place?' Catherine asked.

'What?' I hadn't heard. To me it was Monteith's.

'The Grand Pygmalion. I was down at the music hall last night with my young man, and someone said they thought it was going to be like one of those Eastern bazaars, a bit of everything.'

I started to laugh, stopping it when Miss Adams glared at me from the other end of the floor.

'Why don't you come out with us on Saturday?' Catherine asked impulsively. 'They'll have the new turns on at the halls. I can ask my Jimmy to bring one of his mates if you like. If you don't have someone that is.'

I didn't. I'd broken off with the boy I'd been seeing at the start of the year. I don't know why, but everything he said started to annoy me. And Saturday we'd have our first pay packets.

'All right,' I agreed. 'Why not?' It could be fun after a week of work. My mother wouldn't mind, as long as I wasn't too late home.

And they worked us hard. We earned our money that week, I have to say. Carrying boxes, setting the goods out in the most becoming way. Then doing them over and over after Miss Adams found fault with our work.

By five o'clock on Saturday I was ready for it to end. Everything would be different on Monday, once the customers started coming in. Catherine and I changed out of our uniforms into our best clothes, everything carefully hung in the lockers so it wouldn't crease. She took her time, changing her hairstyle once, then again, until I was afraid the lads would have given up on us.

'Come on,' I chivvied as she put on her cape.

'Always better to keep them waiting,' she told me. 'Just makes them more eager to see you. If you're on time they'll just take you for granted.'

Maybe she thought so; I wasn't as certain.

We met them in one of the gin palaces on Boar Lane, down near the railway stations. Bright lights, the brass and wood all shining, voices loud and happy to be free after a week of labouring. I was introduced to Jimmy. He was good-looking, but in an obvious way. And he knew it, cocky and sure of himself.

His friend, John, was different. Chalk and cheese, the two of them. Quiet, not so talkative. At first I thought this was going to be a waste. But after an hour and a couple of pints he began to smile a bit more.

We stopped for fish and chips then went on to the Pleasure Palace on Lands Lane. Laughed at the comedians, even though half their jokes were as old as my granddad. We had a good singalong and oohed and aahed at the acrobats. Another round of drinks in the intermission.

When it was all done, and Catherine and Jimmy wanted to be off on their own to canoodle, John offered to escort me home.

'It's quite a way to Wortley,' I told him doubtfully. 'And the omnibus goes right to the end of our road.'

But he insisted. It was warm enough to sit on the top deck. Couldn't see the stars, though, just like most nights. Too much soot and haze in the air.

We had a chance to talk. He was a fitter over at Hunslet Engine Company, but he'd scrubbed up well. It was a skilled trade, he told me proudly. He'd finished his apprenticeship and he had his eye on becoming a foreman eventually. Maybe even open his own little shop one day, making specialist parts. There was a future in that.

He was serious, but he liked to smile, too.

He walked me almost to the door. I stopped him going any further. If my mam saw him there'd only be questions later. I wasn't ready for that.

'Do you think…' he began and I waited. 'You know, maybe I could see you again.'

'I'd like that,' I told him.

His eyes widened. I think I'd surprised him.

'Next Saturday?' he asked tentatively.

'All right. Why don't you meet me outside work and we can decide what we want to do.'

Monday morning we had to report to work early. Miss Hardisty and Miss Adams looked us over carefully. No smudges, nothing out of place on our uniforms. Then we all had to parade down to the ground floor where Mr. Montheith was waiting to address us.

'We're here at the start of a remarkable enterprise,' he said. He was smiling widely and almost hopping from one leg to the other, he was that excited. 'There has never been a place like this in Leeds before. We're creating a wonderland of shopping.'

He carried on for another five minutes about this and that, until everyone was fidgeting, just ready for him to open the doors. They'd taken the newspaper off the windows earlier, so pedestrians could see a few of the things we had for sale.

Catherine and I looked at each other, both of us trying not to laugh. If we started we'd never stop.

Finally he was done.

'Ladies and gentlemen, please return to your stations,' Mr. Monteith told us and pulled the watch from his waistcoat. 'We shall open in four minutes.'

I could hear the clank of the lift and the sound of feet on the marble stairs leading up to our floor. A woman in an expensive hat and a fox stole came towards me. I smiled.

'Good morning, madam. How may I help you?'

Historical Note: Monteith, Hamilton and Monteith opened at the junction of Boar Lane and Trinity Street in the 1880s. It was billed as the first department store in Leeds, although that honour might have belonged to the Co-op on Albion Street. But it was certainly the biggest, with four floors and 200 staff. It brought London shopping to Leeds and offered a huge array of goods. It's ironic, perhaps, or maybe simply a continuing thread of history that Trinity Shopping

Centre occupies much the same space today.

Christmas – 1890

'Excuse me, luv, do you have one like that in a plum colour?' Annabelle Harper pointed at the hat on display behind the counter. It was soft blue wool, with a small crown and a wide brim, decorated with a long white feather and trailing lace meant to tie under the chin.

The shop assistant smiled.

'I'm afraid not, madam. We only have what's on display. I'm very sorry.'

'Doesn't matter.' She put down her purchases, stockings, bloomers, garters, and a silk blouse. 'I'll just take those, please.'

Be polite to everyone, that's what her mother had said when she was younger, and it was a rule Annabelle had lived by. It cost nothing, and a little honey always ensured good service.

The Grand Pygmalion was packed with people shopping. Women on their own, with a servant along to carry purchases, wives with long-suffering husbands who looked as if they'd rather be off enjoying a drink somewhere.

Four floors, two hundred people to help the customers, wonderful displays of goods. It just seemed to grow busier and busier each year. But it was the only real department store in Leeds. She waited as the girl totted up the totals.

'I have an account here, luv.'

She saw the quick flicker of doubt and gave a kind smile. Couldn't blame the lass. She didn't sound like the type of person with the money to shop here. Then the gaze took in her clothes and jewellery and the girl nodded. Annabelle had brass.

'Of course, madam. What name is it?'

'Mrs. Annabelle Harper. The address is the Victoria public house on Roundhay Road.'

Everything neatly packed and tied into a box, she walked out on to Boar Lane. A fortnight until Christmas and it was already cold. Bitter. A wind whistled along the street from the west. All around her she could hear people with their wet, bronchitic coughs. It'd probably snow soon enough, she thought.

Omnibuses, trams, carts and barrows moved along the road, a constant clang of noise. On the corner with Briggate, by the Ball-Dyson clock, a Salvation Army brass band was playing, their trumpets and tubas competing against the vehicles and the street sellers crying their goods.

She pulled the coat closer around her body as she walked, clutching the reticule tight in her hand. Plenty of crime this time of year. Married to a detective inspector, she couldn't help but hear about it. And she had enough cash with her for something special; she didn't want to lose that.

As she strolled up towards the Headrow, all the lights in the shops were already glowing. Only three and it was almost dark. Roll on spring, she thought, then stopped herself. Never wish the days away. Who used to say that? She racked her brain. Come on, Annabelle told herself, you're not old enough to forget things yet.

Then it came. Old Ellie Emsworth at Bank Mill. Annabelle was ten, she'd been at the mill two years, working as a doffer, still too young to be on the machines. Six days a week, twelve hours a day for not even two bob a week when all she wanted to be was out there, away from it all. Ellie had worked the loom all her life. She was probably no more than thirty-five but she looked ancient, worn-down.

'I know you don't like it here,' Ellie had said to her one day as they ate their dinner. Bread and dripping for Annabelle, all her family could afford. 'But don't go wishing the days away. They pass quick enough, lass. Soon you'll wish you had them back.'

She smiled. For a moment she could almost hear Ellie's voice, rough as lye soap.

People pressed around her as she walked, some of them smiling with all the joy of the season, others glum and po-faced. Christmas, she thought. They'd never had the money to make a do of it when she was little. As soon as she had a little, when she'd married the landlord of the Victoria, she'd given presents and spent all she could afford.

Even the Christmas after he died, she'd been determined to put on a brave face. A big meal for friends, presents that saw their eyes shine. It made her happy.

And now she had Tom Harper. She had the wedding ring on her finger and she felt happier than she had in a long, long time. This was going to be their first married Christmas and she was going to buy him something he'd never forget. A new suit. A beautiful new suit.

Along New Briggate, across from the Grand Theatre, the buildings were bunched together. Business on top of business as the floors climbed to the sky. Photographers, an insurance agent, gentleman's haberdasher. You name it, it was all there if you looked hard enough.

The girl stood in the doorway of number fifteen, a broken willow basket at her feet. At first Annabelle's glance passed over her. Then she looked again. For a moment she was taken back twenty years. She was ten again and staring at Mary Loughlin. They'd gone to school together, started at the mill together, laughed and played whenever they had chance. The same flyaway red hair that Mary had tried to capture in a sober bun. The same pale blue eyes and freckles over the cheeks. The same shape of her face.

'Wreath, ma'am?' The girl held it out, a poor thing of ivy and holly wrapped around a thin branch of pine. 'It's only a shilling,' she said hopefully.

Her wrist was thin, the bones sticking out, and her fingers were bare, the nails bitten down to the quick, flesh bright pink from the cold. An old threadbare coat and clogs that looked to be too small for her feet.

'What's your name, luv?'

The girl blushed.

'Please ma'am, it's Annabelle.'

For a second she couldn't breathe, putting a hand to her neck. Then, very gently she shook her head.

'Your mam's called Mary, isn't she?'

The girl's eyes widened. She stared, frightened, tongue-tied, biting her lower lip. Finally she managed a nod.

'She was, ma'am, yes.'

'Was? Is she dead?'

'Yes, ma'am. Three year back.'

Annabelle lowered her head and wiped at her face with the back of her gloves.

'I'm sorry, luv,' she said after a while. 'Now, how much are these wreaths?'

'A shilling, ma'am.'

'And how many do you have?'

'Ten.'

She scrambled in her purse and brought out two guineas.

'That looks like the right change to me.' She placed them in the girl's hand. Before she let go of the money, she asked, 'What was your mother's surname before she wed, Annabelle?'

'Loughlin, ma'am.'

'I tell you what. There's that cocoa house just across from the theatre, Annabelle Loughlin. I'd be honoured if you'd let me buy you a cup. You look perished.'

The girl's fingers closed around the money. She looked

mystified, scared, as if she couldn't believe this was happening.

'Did your mam ever tell you why she called you Annabelle?'

'Yes ma'am.' For the first time, the girl smiled. 'She said it was for someone she used to know when she was little.'

Mrs. Harper leaned forward. Very quietly she said:

'There's something I'd better tell you. I'm the Annabelle you're named for.'

She sipped a mug of cocoa as she watched the girl eat. A bowl of stew with a slice of bread to sop up all the gravy, then two pieces of cake. But what she seemed to love most was the warmth of the place. Young Annabelle kept stopping and staring around her, gazing at the people and what they had on their plates.

She was twelve, she said. Two older brothers, both of them working, and two younger, one eight and still at school, the other almost ten and at Bank Mill.

'What does he do there?'

'He's a doffer,' the girl said and Annabelle smiled.

'That's what your mam and I did when we started. Finally I couldn't stand it anymore and went into service.'

'But you're rich,' the girl said, then reddened and covered her mouth with her hand. 'I'm sorry.'

'I've got a bob or two,' she agreed. 'I was lucky, that's all.' The girl finished her food. 'Do you want more?'

'No ma'am. Thank you.'

'And don't be calling me ma'am,' she chided gently. 'It makes me feel old. I'm Annabelle, the same as you. Mrs. Harper if you want to be formal.'

'Yes, Mrs. Harper.'

'What does you da do, luv?'

'He's dead, too.' There was a sudden bleakness in her voice. 'Two years before my mam. So me and Tommy, he's the oldest, we look after everything.'

Annabelle waved for the bill and counted out the money to pay as the girl watched her.

'What work do you do? When you're not selling wreaths, I mean.'

'This and that ma'a— Mrs. Harper.'

'And nothing that pays much?' The girl shook her head. 'You still live on the Bank?'

'On Bread Street.'

'Can you find your way down to Sheepscar?'

'Course I can.' For a second the bright, cheeky spark she remembered in Mary flew.

'Good, because there's a job going if you want one. I own a bakery down there, and someone left me in the lurch.' The girl just looked at her. 'It's not charity, you'll have to work hard and if you skive you'll be out on your ear. But I give a fair day's pay for a fair day's graft. What do you say?'

For a second the girl was too stunned to answer. Then the words seemed to tumble from her mouth.

'Yes. Thank you, ma'am. Mrs. Harper, I mean. Thank you.'

Annabelle looked her up and down.

'If you're anything like your mam you'll be a grand little worker.'

'I'll do my best. Honest I will.'

'I know, luv. You're going to need some new clothes. And I daresay the rest of your lot could use some bits and bobs, too.' She took a five pound from her purse and laid it on the table. 'That should do it.' The girl just stared at the money. 'Don't be afraid of it,' Annabelle told her. 'It won't bite. You buy what you need.'

'Do you really mean it?' The words were barely more than a whisper.

'I do.' She grinned. 'When I saw you, it was like seeing at Mary all over again. Took me right back. You're just as bonny as she was.' She stood, the girl quickly following. 'You be at Harper's Bakery at six tomorrow morning. Mrs. Harding's the manager, tell her I took you on. I'll be around later.'

'Yes, Mrs. Harper. And… thank you again.'

'No need, luv. Just work hard, that's all I ask. You get yourself off to the Co-op and buy what you want.'

The girl had the money clenched tight in her small fist. At the door, before she turned away, she said:

'Mrs. Harper?'

'Yes, luv?'

'Sometime, will you tell me what my mam was like when she was young?'

'You know what? I'd be very happy to do that.'

She watched the girl skip off down the street. Who'd have thought it, Mary calling her lass Annabelle? She shook her head and looked up at the clock. A little after four. She still had time to go to that tailor's on North Street and order Tom a new suit for his Christmas present.

Historical Note: There was no safety net of welfare in the Victorian age. The poor struggled by as best they could. The alternative was the workhouse and it was one few desired. Families were split up and they laboured hard for their keep. Most anything was better than that, even selling wreaths at Christmastime. But a few did find some luck, and what better season for it?

The White Slaves of Leeds - 1896

As the train left Leeds, I looked back to see the pall of smoke covering the city. It was a rich place; rich for some, anyway. We gathered steam, moving south at a good pace and I pulled the sheaf of notes from my briefcase.

I'd talked to a number of people, male and female, for my article. The poor and the poorest, each tale sadder than the last. But it was the faces of the girls that stayed with me. So young and so hopeless. Leeds is a city of many industries, but for the girls there are few options but service or the mills.

I'd been fortunate to have a good contact in Miss Isabella Ford, a Quaker and a socialist who'd long battled for these women, and she'd given me introductions to some of them at the Wholesale Clothiers' Operatives Union. First, though, she'd instructed me on the system the masters implemented for their own advantage.

'There are fines for everything,' Miss Ford told me. 'Unfortunately, thanks to the judges' interpretation of the Truck Act, these are legal. A girl came to me who'd been forced to pay a fine of tuppence, when all she earned that day was a penny-ha'penny. Why? Because she was a minute late to work. The masters employ a boy as timekeeper and his earnings are commission from all the fines levied. Another woman had been deducted two shillings from her week's pay for bad work, when she'd made a total of four shillings and tuppence. But the owners went on to sell the goods as new and she never saw that money back.'

She brought in a girl, Mary Ann, who'd been forced to leave her job in the mill because she couldn't make any money there. She was shy and nervous, wondering if she should even be talking to me, if some vengeance awaited her. I had to assure Mary Ann that I wouldn't name her in the article; only then would she speak.

'How much did you earn in a week?' I asked her.

'In a good week I made two shilling and seven pence, sir,' she told me. 'But often it was less, depending on the work going in the mill. One week it was just a shilling.'

'And what did you have to pay out?' Miss Ford prompted.

'We had to pay for our sewings, the thread and everything else. That week when I only made a shilling, I'd had to spend eight pence. Often it was ten pence.'

'Tell him where you worked,' Miss Ford suggested.

'They called it a punishing house.' The girl reddened as she said the words. 'We hardly had time for our dinner, and the room for it was so small that you could only get a few in there at a time. I never used it. We had to bring our own dinner, but the master charged us a penny or tuppence 'for cook' – to heat it for us, I mean. And you had to pay it, no ifs or buts. Everyone did. When I didn't have enough money, I didn't eat. It was the same with the other girls. Some of them would beg food from the men, but I couldn't. Doing that just led to things.'

Miss Ford told me about more tolls inflicted on the girls. A penny in the shilling for steam power, no matter if the girl worked from home. In some places the girls have to pay a penny or two towards the rent of the factory. Then the masters will round down the wages to an even number, so the odd pennies vanish from the wage packet.

'They promise the girls that the money will go towards a trip for them. But in my years working for the union, I've never heard of a single trip yet.'

The wages vary from season to season, and in slack times many can earn no more than two shillings a week. Even when they're busy it's rare to make more than twelve shillings a week. One or two had made fifteen shillings at times, but they were the quickest, best workers, with full time and overtime.

Often the masters will beat down the prices to line their pockets a little more.

'One time, when we were all very hungry,' a girl called Jane explained, 'the foreman told us there were four hundred sailor suits coming up. Would we do them for threepence each? We refused, because the lowest price should have been threepence-halfpenny. The foreman kept us waiting a day and a half, and at last we were so hungry that we gave in.'

Catherine, a woman who looked to be twenty-five, pinch-faced and sallow, her hair greasy, told me:

'The masters often say they have so many hundred articles to be sewn, if we want to do them at a reduced rate. We prefer not to be idle, so we accept, expecting to have so many to sew. But the masters have lied, and there is much less to sew than had been promised.'

The masters never told them when work would be slack, she said, and the foremen were bullies, using foul language to the girls.

'We come to the factory, and if there's no work, we have to stay in case some comes in. They never tell us so people won't know there's no business.'

Another girl confirmed this to me.

'I come in at eight am,' she told me. 'If I'm late I'll be fined a penny or tuppence. There will be nothing for me to do. Then I'll sit at my machine doing nothing until half past twelve. Then I'll ask the foreman if I can go home. He'll say, 'No, there's orders coming up after dinner.' Dinner? I probably haven't had any, knowing work was slack and expecting to get home. So I go without it. At half-past one I'll go back to my machine and sit doing nothing. Foreman will say: 'Work hasn't come up yet'. I have to sit at my machine. Once I fainted from hunger and asked to be allowed to go home. But they wouldn't let me, and locked me up in the dining room. I sit at my machine till three or four. Then the forman will say, as though he were conferring a favour: 'The orders don't seem to be coming in, you can go home till the morning'. And I go home without having earned a farthing. Sometimes work may come in the afternoon, and then I will stay on till half past six, earning a wage for the last two or three hours.'

Historical Note: Journalist Robert Sheracy travelled around Britain, interviewing people for a series called 'The White Slaves of England', published over a number of issues in 1896 in *Pearson's Magazine*. He did come to Leeds, where he talked to a number of people for the article entitled 'The White Slaves of England: The Slipper-Makers and Tailors of Leeds'. Several of the quotes here are taken directly from the testimony given to him. Their words are more powerful than any fiction.

I Predict A Riot – 1917

The first night took us by surprise. We all knew something was going to happen – everywhere we went in Leeds it seemed as if we'd heard someone saying 'Jew this,' 'Sheeny that,' 'Yid something else.' But we hadn't expected them to come through the Leylands, breaking windows, daubing their hatred in paint on our walls, and ready for a fight. They beat old Mr. Kazinsky until he bled and left him lying on the street.

The baker, the tailors, the little shops on the corners, they looted them all. And it wasn't just a few of them who came; they arrived in their hundreds. As soon as we heard the noise, we dashed out, still in our braces and shirts. We grabbed what we could – sticks, stones, bottles, anything – to defend what was ours.

But the first night we never stood a chance. There were just too many of them. Not only young men, but miners and older folk who should have known better. And where were the police?

They came when it was all over. Of course.

When the morning arrived we counted the cost. Seven in hospital, but they'd all survive, thank God. At least another twenty hurt. More windows broken than people could count. Women worked out on the pavement, heads bowed in sorrow as they swept up the pieces of glass that glinted in the June sun.

'Jews are cowards.'

Someone had painted that, some bastard who could have been on the front line himself, in a trench. Let him tell that to the two brothers of mine who were dead in France or Belgium, or somewhere like that. The War Office had never told us exactly where they fell. Or they could say it to the other Jews who'd joined the Leeds Pals and lost their lives on the Somme last year.

The old folk here felt the fear from the night. They'd seen it before in the pogroms that made them flee their homes and come to England. They believed they'd be safe here. Now they were busy repacking old suitcases, sorting out the little things they wanted to take, preparing for a new journey, a new life somewhere else. A place where hope might grow.

But for the rest of us, Leeds was the only home we'd ever known. We spoke Yiddish, but that was only at home. In town it was all English, sounding as Yorkshire as anyone.

This was our land, too, and we'd be damned if we'd let a

bunch of thugs push us off it. We were proud of the place. I'd even wanted to put on a uniform and fight for the King, but my father wouldn't allow it.

'Moishe and Abraham are dead,' he told me in his slow, sad voice, looking at the photographs of them lovingly displayed on the mantel. 'I'm not going to lose all my sons.'

So while another generation cleared up the debris and trembled, we made our plans. They'd return. If you were Jewish, you knew that; it was deep inside. Once the blood lust rose, they returned. That was history.

We met in the ginnel behind Sam Cohen's sweatshop. There was no sound of sewing machines from inside. People should have been working, but no one had the heart for it today. They were looking ahead and discussing their escape with fearful eyes.

About twenty of us gathered. David was the leader. A good Jewish name for someone in command, I thought. He was eighteen, big and strong, the kind of person who had the kind of quality you just wanted to follow. He wouldn't fight for the flag until they conscripted him, but he'd fight for our piece of this city.

'Ben,' he nodded as he saw me. I was fourteen, but tall for my age, and he could see the anger burning in my eyes. I knew all the faces there. Not just the boys, but the girls, too. This was their battle as much as ours, and everyone was welcome. We didn't even need to say it.

David had his two lieutenants, Isaac and Adam. Isaac was a fat boy with spots on his face who waddled rather than walked. But he had a quick mind. He understood things without even seeming to try, one of those who hardly needed to try in school. And there was Adam. He was a brawler. A year younger than me, but I didn't know anyone who'd dare go up against him. Together, they'd help us win.

'They'll be back tonight,' David said, and we all agreed. 'Isaac's had a few ideas…'

They waited until long after dark, until they'd had time to drink down their courage. I'd been sent down to the bottom of Poland Street to be a lookout. It wasn't dangerous work. I'd grown up here, I knew all the back ways around, and I could run fast. Especially if someone was after me.

In the end I heard them before I saw them. Swearing and shouting, some of them singing 'Tipperary' like an army on its way to war. If you're that keen, join up, I thought bitterly. See how you like the real thing. But they'd be discovering what war was like soon enough.

There were plenty of them, even more than the night before, I could see that. As soon as they came into view I dashed off to give the warning. David issued his instructions. It seemed as if everyone in the Leylands under the age of twenty-five was ready for this. The bastards wouldn't find it so easy tonight.

A few people stayed in view, just as Adam planned it. Enough to tempt them on, but able to scatter quickly before they were hurt. We'd hidden little arsenals everywhere. Rocks, cobbles, stones. Heavy branches that we'd collected from the trees around Meanwood during the afternoon. We were going to use bits of Leeds to defeat them.

Some of our lads darted towards the invaders, tossing stones that deliberately fell short. It was enough to provoke them, to get them chasing the throwers, to draw them into our territory. They sprinted and our boys disappeared, vanishing down tiny entrances, over walls, through houses, until all the *goys* found themselves running along an empty street. The ones in front were halfway down when they began to wonder if something was wrong. Those farther back were busy smashing windows and yelling out their taunts. They weren't thinking of anything but destruction.

We came at them from behind, throwing the rocks first, enough to send them running a little, so they all crowded together. They had their backs to us, turning as soon they heard our boots, some of them going down from the stones. They were armed with sticks, but so were we. And we weren't afraid. We weren't the type who thought that the only way to fight was by terrorising people in the night.

A few of them found their bravery and fought back. More of them were startled and bunching in on each other. They hadn't reckoned on any resistance. In their minds, Jews really were cowards, we didn't fight. But the surprise was only beginning. As they moved away down the street, bedroom windows opened and pans of hot water that the girls had been heating on their stoves were emptied on them. Hot enough to scald. That got them screaming.

One big *goy* had Adam pinned on the ground. He'd raised his stick, ready to bring it down, when my branch hit him hard in the back and he collapsed with a cry. Then we were kicking him, giving him bruises to remember for a few weeks.

There was blood running on pavement and men crouched, nursing their wounds, holding their heads and their arms. Some of theirs, some of ours. But the Jewish boys were quickly bustled away indoors, to any house where they could be tended.

We could hear the police whistles blowing from a quarter of a mile away. That was our signal. We melted away so quickly we might only ever have been a dream. A nightmare. We knew where to run, and before the coppers even arrived we were all back in our own houses, sitting as if nothing had happened.

We hurt, we had wounds, but we'd given better than we got. We'd won.

They ran right into the police when they tried to flee. Plenty arrested. A few unconscious on the cobbles. But no one was likely to die, thank God. No one would have wanted that on their conscience.

The next morning we all met again. No plans this time, but to celebrate. We'd seen them off. There was damage, a few shops looted, some windows broken. But nowhere near as bad as the night before.

We could still see the blood dried on the streets. Some of our boys showed off their injuries, trying to impress the girls.

'They won't be back,' David announced. 'They won't want another beating.'

That night the police were out in force. If they'd done their job properly in the first place, there wouldn't have been a problem. We wouldn't have been forced to become the law.

People still looked at us in town. Some of theirs still spat. There was the odd scuffle. But the riots were over. It might not be peace in France, but it was closer to it in the Leylands.

Historical Note: On the nights of third and fourth of June, 1917, large gangs invaded the Leylands – the area where most of Leeds' Jews lived – in an anti-Semitic riot. They caused plenty of damage, but the Jews did fight back. The estimate from the police is that up to a thousand people were involved. There was no repeat on the third night as the police flooded the area with constables, and no more real incidents to follow.

A Sale of Effects – 1919

Billy Cartwright moved down King Street, leaning heavily on the crutch so the cast barely touched the ground. After a week he had the hang of it and he could swing along almost as quickly as someone walking.

At the Metropole Hotel he eased himself up the stairs. A sign with an arrow stood on an easel – *Leeds City sale* – and he followed along a heavily carpeted corridor to a large room already covered in a fug of smoke. Cups of tea stood on some of the tables, and men in good suits sat puffing on their pipes and talking as they looked through the list of items for sale.

Billy saw a hand go up and Fred Linfoot waved him over. All the players had gathered together at the back, crowded around three large tables. The auction hadn't begun yet but the ashtrays were already full, cigarette butts crushed down together.

'How long before the cast's off?' John Sampson asked.

'A fortnight,' Billy answered. The broken leg was stretched out, the crutch lying on the floor, out of the way. He glanced around. There were men here from every club in the league, older and with serious faces. Prosperous men who sat straighter as the auctioneer approached his lectern. It was time for business and that was why they'd come to Leeds.

A Sale of Effects, the notice had read. Only four words. Billy had seen the advertisement in the *Yorkshire Post*, scarcely believing four words could take in so much. Metropole Hotel, 17th October, conducted by S. Whittam and Sons. He'd looked at it again and again before he'd pushed the paper away. Another hour or so and it would be as if Leeds City had never existed. Even the goal netting and the balls would be sold off. The players auctioned like they were slaves.

He knew who'd fetch the best price – Billy McLeod. He was the best footballer by far, the one everyone would want. He sat quietly, listening to the conversations around him.

It was all a stupid bloody mess and if it hadn't been for Charlie Copeland they wouldn't be here today. The way he understood it, if Charlie hadn't reported the club to the FA for paying players during the war, none of this would have happened. Or if Leeds had been willing to produce its books when it was asked. Instead, the chairman had refused and they'd all paid the price. Kicked out of the League, wound up, everything must go.

There'd be more to it, Billy thought. There always was, wheels within wheels, and someone would have made a few quid. They always did, although none of it would come down to them on the sharp end.

The auctioneer banged the gavel and the room was suddenly silent and alert. He was going to start with the players, the club's most important asset, he said, some short speech about how sad this occasion was, the end of an era.

Billy's mouth was dry. Everything rested on this. He'd be happy if someone offered two hundred pounds for him. Even a hundred. Just fifty. Anything to keep him playing.

The problem was that he'd never run out for the club. He only turned eighteen during the summer and signed for the club in September. Then, during the second week of training there'd been the tackle. As soon as it happened, he knew. It was all he could do not to yell and start crying like a kid. A broken tibia, that was what the doctor said after they'd driven him to the Infirmary. Six weeks in plaster. And after that it'd be a good three months before he'd be fit again, the muscle built back up and ready. In the New Year – if he was lucky.

They'd been the worst weeks of his life. Cooped up at home every day, just his mam for company while his father and his brothers went off to work. No brass in his pocket. Limping down to Elland Road for the home matches, wishing for time to pass until it could be him out there.

He was good enough. He had to believe he was. He'd played inside right for Leeds Schoolboys until he left when he was fourteen, and then he'd been in the works team at Blackburn's, the Olympia Works up on Roundhay Road. Saturday mornings off, paid, to play up on Soldiers' Field. It hadn't been a bad life. The old factory that had once been a roller skating rink was fun, a good bunch to work with.

But he'd known he wasn't going to stay. At fifteen he tried to join up, to follow his brother into the Leeds Pals. A worn-out sergeant told him to come back when he was old enough. He did, a year later, an altered birth certificate tight in his fist. A week later he was in Catterick, learning what it meant to be a Tommy.

By December of 1917 he'd been in France for six weeks. He was already scared, sick and dirtier than he could have believed. Half of those he'd known in training were already dead, He was numb inside, just living from hour to hour. After a week in the trenches he'd wondered if he'd ever feel warm and dry again. After three weeks, he didn't care as long as he lived to the end of this war and he could know some silence again.

Come Armistice Day he had no idea where he was. It was simply another muddy hole in another muddy, lifeless landscape. It could have been in France, Belgium or Germany. He didn't know and it didn't matter. The important thing was they could put down their guns and not worry about being killed.

He could look forward to a hot bath, Billy thought, and going home. Looking around, he could see the same thought in every pair of eyes.

He ended up walking halfway to the coast. The transport never arrived and after waiting for three days the brigadier gave up and ordered them to start on foot. It was a slow march. They were all eager to be back in Blighty, but they were weary, half-fed creatures. The leather of Billy's boots had rotted away in places, he had trench foot; each step took effort. The further they travelled from the front, the more they seemed to be walking into a dream of green fields and houses that hadn't been demolished by shells. The type of places they'd almost forgotten existed.

He wasn't in Leeds for Christmas. He'd spent that in hospital while they tended his feet. He hobbled home in January, his mother's arms around him as soon as he was through the front door. Not his oldest brother, though. He'd never come back.

Billy was still thin, still weak. He wasn't even eighteen yet and he'd seen enough death for seven lifetimes. His ma made him beef tea three times a day and forced as much food as he could manage down him. He started back at Blackburn's and began training for the works team again. He ran after work and cut down to ten Woodbines a week.

Before the end of the season he was the first choice for inside right again, more reckless now, as if he knew there was nothing in the game that could scare him. He tackled hard, he ran and he scored, three goals in five games.

The summer, with no matches, left him restless, too full of energy but with nothing to do until his birthday and his trial for Leeds City. He kept up the running, taking off after work for a circuit of Roundhay Park, along by the big lake, through the gorge and back before catching the bus home. Saturday afternoons, with no football to watch, he'd try to cajole workmates into a kick around, something to keep his skills sharp.

Until the day of trial for Leeds he'd been confident. For too long people had told him he was a good footballer. He was always the best in any team. But the others taking part were his equals. Some were better, he had no doubt about that. They made him sweat, made him play, made him think. And when it was over, for the first time he had to wonder if he was good enough.

For the next three days he was on edge, going straight home from work to see if there'd been any post for him. When it finally arrived he let it sit in his hand, as if its weight might tell him what was inside. It took courage to open the envelope, and he had to breathe hard before unfolding the letter.

Dear Mr. Cartwright…

He read it through twice to be certain he was right. They were taking him on at three pounds a week. For the rest of the evening he couldn't stop smiling, then couldn't rest in his bed although he had to work in the morning. He gave his notice, and by the start of September he was training every day at Elland Road with the men he'd only cheered from the terraces. More than that, he was playing against them and just beginning to understand how much he had to learn. He wasn't good; he'd barely even started.

The divot shouldn't have been there. They all said that later. But he'd been chasing down a long pass, watching the ball, not the pitch. His studs caught and he went down awkwardly. Barely two weeks into his professional career and he'd broken his leg.

Each club offered a sealed bid for the players they wanted. Billy wasn't surprised when McLeod went for £1,250. He outclassed everyone else in the side. Glancing over, he could see the mix of pride and relief on the man's face. Then it was Harry Millership and John Hampson, a thousand each. And then it was down the line – eight hundred, six hundred, five – all the way to Frank Chipperfield, off to Sheffield Wednesday for a hundred. That left seven of them looking worriedly at each other. The auctioneer coughed. Four had new clubs. No fee. No one for Mick Sutcliffe, Charlie Foley. Or for him.

By the time he was listening again, they were selling off the goal posts and the nets. He pushed himself up, leaning heavily on the crutch, and made his way out, threading through the tight spaces between tables. None of the men from other clubs bothered to look up at him.

Out in the corridor he stopped to light a cigarette. As he was about to move off again, he heard a man say:

'Billy.'

He turned. The manager was there, Mr. Chapman, the one who'd picked him out from the trial. Just like Leeds City, he'd been banned from football, that was what Billy had heard, although the rumour was that he was going to appeal. He was growing heavy at the waist, the start of jowls on his face. He gave a sad smile.

'Yes, boss?'

'I just wanted to tell you I'm sorry, lad. I had a word with them, said you had potential. But they didn't want to take a chance.' He shrugged slightly.

'Thank you, boss.'

'Don't give up. You have talent. Keep trying, all right?'

'Yes, boss. Thank you.'

He turned and hobbled away.

Historical Note: In 1919, eight games into the season, Leeds City was wound up by the Football Association over alleged illegal payments to players during the First World War. Ordered to produce their books, the club refused, forcing the FA to take action. If they'd done as requested, Leeds might have been fined – what they did was no worse than most other clubs in those wartime years – but they'd probably have escaped greater punishment. As it was, everything that belonged to the club, even the players, was sold by auction in October 1919, and their fixtures taken over by Port Vale. A year later Leeds did return, but as Leeds United Football Club, whose glory days of the 1960s and 1970s, under the management of Don Revie, remain tales of joy for fans.

Jenkinson's Bug Van – 1934

'This it, then?' the woman asked. She stood with her arms folded, standing back from the house. Far down the street a man pushed a handcart, piled with furniture, stopping every few yards to wipe his face with a handkerchief. Then another cart came round the corner, drawn by a weary old horse.

I stared at them for a moment. Wouldn't give a tanner on the winner, I thought and smiled.

'Aye, it's alright, is this,' she concluded with a sharp nod. 'This one mine, is it?'

Bob looked at his notebook. He was a dapper man, shirt and tie always just so, hair Brylcreemed under his cap, the brown coat clean every day, never a button missing, always a twinkle in his eye when he was talking to the women. Not that he'd have done anything if one of them had been willing. He'd have run a mile.

'If you're Mrs. Cooper, it is. Three bedrooms.'

'That's me, luv.' She was a bony woman, all sharp knuckles and skinny calves. It was June, the sun shining, but she was still wearing a wool coat, buttoned up, and boots rather than shoes. She nodded down the street. 'That's me fella there, and the lads and my lass are on are Josh Hartnett's wagon.' She glanced around. 'Dun't look like there are many living here yet.'

'Not yet,' I told her. 'But they're all coming.' This was the third street we'd done on the new Gipton estate. By dribs and drabs it was starting to fill up. Another month and it would really seem alive, children playing, women gossiping outside the shops. 'From Holbeck?'

'Aye,' she said suspiciously. 'How'd you know?' She had a thin face, that look of someone who'd never had enough to eat in her life, her cheeks sunk where half the teeth had been pulled.

'Most of them coming here are from Holbeck,' I told her with a grin. 'Happen you'll see some you know.'

'Like as not,' she agreed with a sniff. 'Not bad round here, is it?' She reached out tentatively and touched one of the bricks. 'Nice and clean.'

'Brand new, that is,' Bob said, as if it wasn't obvious. 'Got everything you need, too. Lovely, bathroom, hot and cold water, gas for cooking. Even a garden at the back for the kiddies. Better than where you were, luv, that's a fact.'

'Mebbe,' Mrs. Cooper said doubtfully.

I'd seen those streets in Holbeck, the ones they were tearing down. Eight back-to-backs in a block, all of them sharing a single privy. Houses full and rats and God only knew what. 'Not fit for human habitation,' the demolition notices read and it was true. Always smoke in the air from all the factories around. Out here there'd be fresh air, grass where the children could play. A sense of the future.

'Are you sure this is the right house?' Mrs. Cooper asked. 'Dun't look like we can afford owt like this.'

'Five bob a week. That's what it says here,' Bob told her and she nodded slowly. It was probably the same they'd paid for their old house.

'You'll like it out here,' I added.

'No offence, luv, and bless you, but you're no more than a babby. You'd not know what we like.'

I blushed. I was sixteen. I'd been working for two years now. Bob laughed.

'He's very sensitive about it,' he said, reaching across and plucking off my cap to ruffle my hair. Mrs. Cooper joined his laughter.

'Don't you worry. I wun't saying owt by it.' She touched my arm and smiled gently. 'You meant well.'

I did mean well. She'd love Gipton; I knew the land round here. When I was younger, my dad and I used to come out here with his gun and shoot rabbits. It was all farmland, no more than a short walk from where we lived in Harehills. My dad had been in the Leeds Pals during the war – he still put on his uniform and marched down the Headrow with them every Remembrance Day – and he'd trained as a sharpshooter. He was careful to make every bullet count, just the way they'd taught him in France. Whenever we went out, only two or three times a year, we'd bring home enough coneys to feed us and all the neighbours for a week. But they'd all be gone now, I supposed, their warrens bulldozed under for all the new houses. For a moment I wondered where they'd find a new home.

The man with the cart was just fifty yards away now, the horse and wagon very close behind. At this rate it would be a tie. And it was debatable who looked more worn out.

'You'll be wanting the keys, luv,' Bob said. 'And the rent book.'

'I will,' the woman agreed. 'Is that what you two do all day, then, welcome folk and hand that out?'

'There's a bit more to it than that,' Bob told her, giving me a glance to shut up. I wasn't going to say anything, anyway. He was better at this.

'Oh aye?' Mrs. Cooper asked. 'Just put it down there,' she ordered her husband. 'We'll tek it all inside in a minute.'

They were the opposite of Jack Sprat and his wife, she like a knobby twig, him large and larded, sweating so much that the cotton of his shirt was soaked. He was bent over, palms resting on his knees, catching his breath. Bob nodded at Josh Hartnett, sitting happily on the wagon as the kiddies clambered down. He'd been out here so often in the last fortnight that his nag could probably find its way without help.

'Right,' said Mrs. Cooper and held out her hand. 'Keys.'

'There's something we have to do first,' Bob said.

'What's that?' she asked warily.

'I need to you put everything in the van.'

'You what?' Her eyes widened and her voice rose as she looked towards the van we'd parked at the kerb, plain dark green with the Leds Corporation crest on the doors. 'What for?'

'Fumigation,' he answered and took a small step backwards.

'Fumi-what?' It took her a moment to understand, then she was ready to explode. 'What are you saying, you cheeky bugger? That my stuff isn't clean?'

'Nothing like that,' Bob answered hurriedly. Two days earlier I'd had to take hold of a woman before she could slap his face. 'It's Councillor Jenkinson's orders. Everything has to go through the van before it can go in the new house, that's all. It's the same for everyone.'

She softened as soon as he mentioned Charlie Jenkinson's name. They all did that. Every one of the women loved him. More than that, they respected him. If it hadn't been for for him on the housing committee, none of these places would have been built and they'd still be living in Holbeck with all the cockroaches, the bedbugs and the rats.

'Aye, well,' she said after a moment, and I knew we'd won. She wouldn't put up more of a fight. The magic name worked on most of them. There was one woman who cursed us blind and her husband had raised his fists, but they were rare. We had to threaten to withhold their rent book before they calmed down.

Mrs. Cooper turned to her husband. 'Right, you can start putting it all in the van. These two will help you.'

It wasn't really part of our job but we always did it, anyway. It wasn't as if any of them had much. A heavy bed, a table and wooden chairs, maybe a worn, cushioned easy chair and a suitcase or two of clothes. Load up, close the doors, start the engine and turn on the gas in the back. Run it for a quarter of an hour then open the vents on the roof. Another five minutes and it was all done. A routine, and we had it down by now. Then pull everything out again and let them see the dead insects littering the floor of the van. They never made any more fuss after that. It was a reminder of the life they were leaving behind. Most of them thanked us.

I started the engine and turned the switch, waiting until I heard the first hiss of the gas and checked my watch. It was too lovely a day to be anywhere but outdoors.

'You know,' Bob was telling the woman, 'they've come up with a scheme now.'

'What's that, then?' she asked, on guard as if he was trying to sell her insurance or something she didn't want and couldn't afford.

'It's the council's idea,' he explained. 'You can buy new furniture and things for the house on tick. A few pennies a week on your rent, that's all.'

She bridled. 'Are you saying what we have isn't good enough? Is that it?'

'No, love, of course not. But they just thought that maybe people would like to start over once they're in a new house.' He gave her one of his smiles, lopsided and charming. 'You know.'

'We'll see. Once we're settled.' And she folded her arms again, waiting.

I opened the back doors. Bob and I helped with the heavy pieces, easing out a thick oak table that had to be fifty years old, the wood filled with scars and stains. Finally everything was on the front lawn. Mrs. Cooper stared inside the empty van for a moment, not saying a word, weighing the keys to the new house in her hand.

'Let's get this lot inside,' she announced finally. 'We don't want to display everything to the new neighbours.' Her husband and the children moved quickly, picking up what they could. She turned to us. 'Well?' she asked. 'Are you going to help or just stand there gawping all day?'

Historical Note: The people of Leeds owe the Rev. Charles Jenkinson a great deal. After moving to Leeds to be a vicar in Holbeck, he was elected as a Labour councillor. When they were voted into power in Leeds in 1933, he became head of the housing committee, and dedicated to building those homes fit for heroes that had never materialised after the First World War – as well as demolishing the slums. Under his leadership new estates were built, the first at Gipton, with rents pegged to income, a revolutionary concept. But, before the old furniture could be moved into a new house, it had to be defested in a council van, which became known locally as Jenkinson's Bug Van. The council did also introduce a hire purchase plan that let tenants buy new furniture and linen on hire purchase, adding a little each week to their rent.

Battle of Holbeck Moor – 1936

We had the word well ahead of time. It was in the newspapers, gossip all through the pubs. On the walk to work in the morning, men would be talking about it. The Blackshirts are coming. Bloody well let them come, I said, and we'll show them what Leeds is about.

I knew why Mosley wanted his fascist scum here. Jews. We have plenty of them, and good people they are, too. A lot of them have moved out to Chapeltown now, them as has some money, any road. But you'll still find enough down in the Leylands, the ones who haven't made a bob or two. Take a walk out along North Street and look at the names over the shops. Do nobody any harm and they work hard, the way a man should.

The Watch Committee spent the week hemming and hawing. Mosley and his gang wanted to have their march right by the Leylands. That'd be a recipe for disaster. Bad enough as it was, with swastikas and slogans painted on the windows of Jewish shops during the night. The fascists said it wasn't them as done it, but we all knew the truth. Too scared to show their faces and try it in the day. Nowt like that had happened since the riots back in '17.

Now me, I was a Communist then. I'm not today, not since the war when I heard about what Stalin did to his people. But I hated fascists with a bloody passion. I knew what was coming with Hitler; anyone with half a brain did. And I didn't want it in my country. Definitely not my bloody city.

Finally them as are supposed to lead us told Mosley and his lot that they couldn't go near the Leylands. Not that they couldn't march, mind you. They could still do that, just not there. Once that order was out, we began making our plans. They were aiming for a big rally on Holbeck Moor, a thousand or more of them. Probably some supporters, too. We knew what we had to do. We were going to make the bastards wish they'd never heard of Leeds.

Didn't take much to put the word about. A nod here, a little natter in the pub of an evening and we knew we'd have a crowd. At first we thought we'd line the route out from town, but that was only going to be a waste of time. Better to meet them up on Holbeck Moor where they were going to have their do.

Now, maybe that was the right decision and maybe it weren't. I heard later that there were plenty of Blackshirts down Meanwood Road. Too bloody close to the Leylands for my liking. Happen we should have had a few of our lads there.

Of course, the party officials talked to the people from the Labour Party. The way I heard it is that the Labour bods spent most of the meeting sucking on their pipes and making sympathetic noises before saying they wouldn't take part in the protests. Soft as bloody butter, the lot of them. Not that it would stop plenty of folk as voted that way. They'd be out there. You give in to fascists once and next time they want a mile more.

The weather was good that morning. Sunny, warm, not much of a hint of a breeze. The 27th of September, 1936. We were all in a good mood as we traipsed up to the Moor. It was going to be a good laugh, and if a few heads got broken, well, it was no more than they deserved, was it?

Half a dozen of us went from our street. I was with Stan. He was a pipe fitter, a strong lad. We'd been mates since we were boys. Went to school together, primary and on. He bought it during the war, out in Burma. All his wife got were a medal. I daresay his body's out there still, somewhere in the jungle.

The closer we got to the place, the more noise we could hear. I'd expected plenty of people, but not like that. Thousands upon thousands, and not enough coppers in view to keep order. Which was exactly what we'd hoped.

Stan gave me a big grin and opened his hand to show some knuckle dusters.

'You'd better watch out,' I warned him. 'The rozzers catch you with those and you'll be up for having an offensive weapon.'

'Nay,' he laughed. 'Come on, Roy, I'm not bloody daft. Any chance of that and I'll drop them.' He was a big lad. Topped six foot, shoulders on him like a bloody barn. He didn't need anything. Just his fists would do enough damage. But he had his ire up, same as the rest of us.

There were runners out, bringing messages on the march.

'They're on Calverley Street,' went around, then, 'they've crossed over the river.'

It was going to be a battle, but we were all in a good mood. Laughing, joking, some singing and chanting. It was like being at the football in some ways. But not others. Plenty of the lads had organised well. They must have spent every evening scouring around, because they had a big arsenal of stones for us to throw.

'Stuff 'em in your jackets, lads,' one man cried. He had a battered bowler hat on his head and a muffler wrapped round his throat, never mind that it was a beautiful day. 'Once they arrive you know what to do.'

There was a mood of anticipation. A celebration. We were going to enjoy ourselves and chase the buggers out of here. The Blackshirts had some supporters already up on the moor, a couple of thousand and more, but we easily outnumbered them ten to one. They didn't look too happy but they didn't dare back down. Not now, before their precious leader even showed his face. But you could see it, they were scared. They knew they were going to get a pasting.

A few of them were hard lads. That was all right. We had ammunition. When someone's chucking rocks at you there's not much you can do but duck and hope for the best. And I reckoned that among the stones the boys must have taken up half the cobbles in Holbeck. Oh yes, we were going to make the buggers hurt.

'They're coming!' The words ran around the crowd. We were all craning our necks to see. Then I spotted them, like a thin river of black, moving slowly. The noise grew as they grew closer. A few cheering, many more of us yelling out insults.

They'd built a podium, a stage of sorts, for Mosley and a few of his cohorts. We waited until he took his place, his little army in front of him, gathered loyally. As soon as he moved forward to open his mouth, we struck up 'The Red Flag', a huge chorus of voices to drown him out. It wasn't planned, it felt natural, but we sang as long and loud as Welshmen at one of their Eisteddfods.

As soon as it died down, the stones started. They arced over our heads and we watched them come down. One of them hit Mosley and made him move back. That brought cheers and a few more rocks.

Some came back at us. It was bound to happen. One or two of our lads were bleeding, but it was never an equal fight. It was a Sunday, and this was our church. The coppers couldn't do much. They tried to keep some order, but they wanted to have their heads down, too, and I can't blame them.

I'd lost sight of Stan in the crowds. He'd waded forward as soon as he could, yelling and screaming, his blood up. God only knew what he'd end up doing.

There were missiles flying backwards and forwards, people crying out. Whenever Mosley tried to speak, 'The Red Flag' began again to drown out his words. It was a good way to feel strong, Communists, Jews, good people from all over Leeds gathering to tell the Blackshirts what we thought of fascism here. We didn't want owt to do with it.

A stone hit me on the shoulders, hard enough but no damage

done. I picked it up and tossed it back. When I looked around I could see everyone had the fire in their eyes. We were here to do a job and we weren't going to leave until it was finished.

Another stone hit Mosley in the face and he fell. Good luck or good aim, I don't know. But we cheered. It gave us heart and we began to push forward.

'Get 'em on the run, lads,' someone shouted and we all laughed. But we all moved forward anyway.

I've no idea how long it lasted. It just seemed like moments but it must have been a lot longer. I was too young to have fought in the Great War but it must have felt like that. Time seemed to speed up and slow down at the same time. It was like electricity was going through me, I could have shocked anyone I touched.

A couple of times I caught the toff's voice, but as soon as anyone heard it we began singing. Sir Oswald, that was his title. Should have been hung for treason. We weren't about to give him much of a chance. Rubbish like his doesn't deserve an airing.

Finally he gave up. This was a battle he didn't have any chance of winning and he knew it. He lined up them as supported him and they began to march away as if they'd won something. But they'd got nowt.

We jeered and shouted until we were hoarse and they couldn't hear us any more. We'd bloody won. Men were laughing their heads off, full of victory. We'd sent them off with their tails between their legs. Someone passed a hip flask around and we all had a nip. It burned on the way down but by God, it felt good.

It was in the newspapers the next day. Well, a few of them. The local ones, which said there'd been thirty thousand on the moor. I don't know if that's true; when you're part of it you can never tell. Certainly the biggest crowd I've ever seen. Biggest I'll ever be part of, I'm sure of that. Most of the large dailies didn't bother to cover it. After all, we're the north, we don't matter. Funny, though, they were quick enough to write up what happened down in London a week later. The Battle of Cable Street, they called it, when all those Cockneys and Jews down there told the fascists what they thought of them, too.

Up here, the magistrates bleated in the press about public order and how terrible it had all been. Stood up on their hind legs and said their piece. But there were only three people arrested. It wasn't as if there was a shortage of candidates to be nicked. Three. It was just a token.

When they appeared in court, all they got was a slap on the

wrist. Someone must have had a word – send them down and there'll be riots. There would have been, too. It was the wisest thing they could have done. The only thing. We'd made the whole bloody city tremble. They might not have shown it, but the council was scared. The law was terrified.

But by God, we showed them. And good on them Londoners for what they did, too. It was a lovely feeling last year when we made our way back off the moor, comrades together. The Battle of Holbeck Moor, someone named it. And that's not bad. But it's not quite the truth. It wasn't a battle, it was a rout. A complete bloody rout.

Historical Note: The Battle of Holbeck Moor did happen. The Watch Committee did refuse Mosley permission to march by the Leylands, but a thousand Blackshirts did go out to Holbeck Moor to hear him speak, where they were met with plenty of protesters. There was plenty of violence, and Mosley was hit by a stone. But it's true that in the end only three people were arrested, out of an estimated crowd of 30,000, and the sentences given were very light.

Tiger, Tiger - 1941

Jack had the shelter built at the bottom of the garden right after Mr. Chamberlain came back from Munich. I used to stand in the back bedroom and watch the men digging out the ground then laying the bricks and putting on the concrete roof.

'When Hitler comes we'll be safe now,' he said. 'And we won't have to share it with anyone.'

He was wrong about that. But then Jack was wrong about most things; the only time I can remember him being right was building the shelter. Even then we didn't need it. No bombs dropped in these suburbs of Leeds. We had a few raids, but nothing like those poor people down in London. I can't imagine how they stood it.

Whenever the siren went off, everyone in the street would come into our shelter. None of them had built one; they'd more sense than brass, I suppose. Jack had signed up to do his bit. God only knew where he was – the only thing he'd managed to get past the censor was that he had brown knees. He could have been in Filey for all I knew.

So it was me and Michael for the duration. But he was at school during the day, and after that he was off with his pals, pretending to machine gun every Nazi and win the war by himself. But once that siren wailed he was down in the shelter and as scared as the rest of us.

I had a job three mornings a week at the museum on Park Row. It might not have been assembling shells or putting Spitfires together, but it was a little something. I enjoyed it, working there with Miss Woods and Mr. Johnson, who was too old to fight and knew all about history. He'd given me a proper tour of the exhibits one day, even telling me about the history of the Indian stuffed tiger that stood inside the doorway and the Egyptian mummy at the top of the stairs. He claimed he could read the hieroglyphics but I wasn't sure I believed him. More than that, working took me out and around people, into all the whirl and bustle of town.

From the bus I'd seen some of the damage the early raids did, all that wreckage at Marsh Lane Station, and it made me shudder. I'd thought we were safe, but the truth was that if a bomb landed on the shelter we might as well have been hiding under cardboard.

Michael was already in bed when the siren sounded. It was right on the stroke of nine, and for a moment my heart stopped, the way it always did when I heard that sound. In less than a minute he was down in the kitchen, socks, slippers and dressing gown over his pyjamas. I'd been listening to the wireless, one of those dance bands that sound like everyone else.

It was March. Outside, the sky was very clear, so many stars up there, and terribly cold.

'Stay right there,' I told Michael, and dashed back into the house for our overcoats. Over the next quarter of an hour the neighbours drifted in. We talked for a while until all the gossip had been given out and we all knew which butcher might have mince the next day. There was a primus stove in the shelter, but it didn't give out much heat. The oil lamps helped, at least we could see each other.

After an hour and a half we'd run out of things to say. Shivers kept running through me from the cold. We were ready for the all-clear to sound, to go back to our beds and warm up. But there was only silence. Then I heard something off in the distance, like a hum. And more. They were coming.

It seemed like we were down there forever. After a while it became apparent that they were targeting the city centre and old Mr. Henderson from number eleven climbed on the roof of the shelter to give us a running commentary. He was sixty if he was a day but he was still active and in the Home Guard.

'Those are incendiaries,' he announced with a shout. 'I can see them burning.' And later, when the planes seemed to come wave after wave and the soft crump of bombs was a constant sound, he'd cry out, 'That must have done some damage,' until we all clambered out to join him.

A little after three we were all back in our houses. Michael trudged up to bed, the poor lamb could hardly keep his eyes open, but I couldn't sleep. It had been like a thousand Guy Fawkes' nights all in one, all light and fire and explosions. Except there was nothing fun about this. There was just terror and destruction and death.

I thought about the museum, hoping it had survived. And then I thought about Jack, somewhere in the world with his brown knees and I lay in bed and cried quietly until the alarm clock went off.

The bus could only go as far as Buslingthorpe Lane before the wardens stopped it. I wasn't going to give up. Instead I walked into town. Quarry Hill Flats had taken a hit and there was smoke still coming from the roof of the market, with water running down

George Street. The air smelt like gunpowder and I had to tread carefully around the rubble.

'You'd best watch yourself, luv,' one of the auxiliary firemen told me. 'There's stuff here that could come tumbling down on you.'

I smiled at him and walked on. There seemed to be plenty like me, people on their way to work, hoping there'd still be a business standing, and those who simply needed to see what the Germans had done to us. It seemed bad, but nothing like the newsreels, where street after street in London had been blown to nothing. If this was our Blitz then we'd come off lightly.

As soon as I turned on to Park Row I could see something was wrong. There was a huge hole in the road, a crater, and I started to walk faster, almost running down the pavement. I could see Miss Woods in the distance, holding something to her face. She was a spinster, fifty-three years old – she was always very exact – with some small private income. She worked at the museum because she wanted to, not because she needed the money. She was the first in and the last to leave every day, caring for the place as if it was her own home. I watched as she bent down and picked something up.

The whole front of the building had gone, as if a giant petulant child had swept his hand across and crushed it. Stone, glass and wood were all scattered across the street, fallen into the hole and all around it. Men stood around, one or two in their ARP helmets, most just in caps, staring, pointing and talking.

Miss Woods seemed to be in shock when I looked at her, dazed, her eyes quite blank. She held up her hand and I could see what she'd rescued from the ground, a piece of old, dirty linen. At first I didn't know what to make of it. Then I took in all the gaping frontage of the museum, the staircase little more than splinters now, and I realised it must have come from our mummy. It might be all that was left of him.

Everything I could see inside the building was blackened. Even the air seemed charred and dead. The desk where I worked didn't exist any more, only a space on the burned and buckled floor where it had once been.

The tiger, I thought. But he was gone, too, not even a scrap of fur. It had all gone. Everything had gone. There was nothing they could shore up, they couldn't make do with what was left. The museum was gone. I put my arm around Miss Woods' shoulders. For a moment the contact seemed to startle her and she began to pull away. I smiled at her gently.

'I know,' I told her. 'I know.'

Historical Note: During World War II, Leeds suffered far less than most industrial cities. There were very few raids, and the only one that did much damage happened in March 1941. At that time Leeds Museum stood on Park Row, and was home to an Egyptian mummy and a stuff tiger from India, among many other things. A German bomb did take out the front of the museum and the tiger was destroyed, along with the mummy. Thankfully, very few lives were lost in the raids on Leeds. The museum is now in the old Civic Theatre, previously the Mechanics' Institute.

Beat Music - 1963

'Are you going?'

'Don't be daft. Of course I'm going.' He hesitated. 'If we can still get tickets.'

They were walking along Duncan Street, past Rawcliffe's with all the neat, clean school uniforms in the window, crossing Briggate and out along Boar Lane.

'There'll be tickets, they only went on sale half an hour ago,' James told him. 'They won't have sold out yet.'

'Hope not.' His fist was curled around the pound note in his pocket. Before taking the bus into Leeds he'd queued for ten minutes to draw it from his Post Office account. His father had disapproved, of course, wasting all that money on a pop concert. But it was just one more criticism on top of so many in the last year.

It was May, almost summer, and the air was warm enough to leave his windbreaker unzipped, the old grey school shirt underneath.

They turned by the station, down onto Bishopgate Street, through the tunnel under the tracks, bricks black and sooty, all the sound amplified. Now they were close to the Queen's Hall he speeded up, his steps tapping quickly on the pavement.

'Did I tell you what my uncle did?'

James glanced over at him, keeping pace easily, wearing a striped tee shirt, a pair of American jeans his father had brought back from a trip, and his plimsolls. He looked relaxed, bemused by the whole idea of spending a little over ten bob to see a group.

'What?'

'You know he's a commercial traveller?'

'Yes.'

'He was up in Sunderland last week, at the hotel where he always stays and sitting in the bar with the other salesmen. You'll never guess who was staying there and came walking in.'

'Go on,' Chris said with a smile. 'You're dying to tell me, anyway.'

'Only the Stones.'

'What, the Rolling Stones?'

James nodded and continued,

'My uncle and the others took one look at them and went off to talk to the manager. They said they weren't going to stay in a place that let in animals. Either the Stones went or they did, and they were the ones who came back week after week.'

'Are you serious?' Chris was close to laughter, his soft smirk cracking into a grin. 'What happened?'

'The manager kicked out the Stones.'

'Bloody hell.'

The words came out as astonishment. James followed his gaze and saw why. There were hundreds of people queueing outside the Queen's Hall, all the way down the side of the building.

'We're going to be here all day trying to get a ticket.'

'Worth it, though.' And it would be if he could get to see the Beatles. He hadn't managed to buy a ticket for their show at the Odeon, but this would be bigger and better. They were even going to be onstage twice during the night. Any money, any length of time spent queuing would be worthwhile. 'Going to stay?'

'I don't know,' James answered doubtfully. 'I said I'd be home by dinnertime to revise for my exams.'

Chris shrugged.

'Your loss. Take a look.'

'What?'

'Girls. Lots of them.' He grinned and pushed his quiff into place, the scent of Brylcreem on his hands, then began to walk to the end of the line. 'But if you want to go, it's OK. I don't mind.'

In the end it only took an hour and a half to move to the ticket window. James tried to chat up the girls around them, but they weren't interested; all they cared about was seeing the Beatles and he wasn't John, Paul, Ringo, or the other one. In the end there'd been nothing to do but enjoy the sunshine and wait.

Chris bought his ticket, paid and began to turn away, when James said,

'One for me, too.'

'I thought you didn't care about the music,' Chris said as they walked back towards Briggate.

'I don't,' he insisted briskly, and it was true. For all his casual appearance, James was the perfect grammar school pupil. Piano to grade six, always at the top of his year, certain to do well in his O-levels next month. Then there'd be a smooth passage through the sixth form all the way to Cambridge. A boy to fulfil all his father's aspirations.

They'd known each other since primary school. On the second day James had stopped Chris from hitting a girl who'd bitten his arm. They'd been friends ever since, a curious bond that neither of them really understood.

It would change soon enough, Chris knew that. He'd sit his exams then leave school. His father already had a job lined up for him, clerking in an office. The two of them would spend less time together, drifting apart. Probably in weeks rather than months. Somewhere in the future they'd bump into each other, say hello, and wonder how they'd ever been close in the first place.

'Did you see how many were still waiting?' James asked.

Chris shook his head.

'There must have been at least another thousand behind us. It's going to be something.' He shrugged. 'I thought I might as well see it.'

'You'll hate it. It'll be loud. And all those girls who were there, they'll be screaming. That's what they do for the Beatles.'

'Maybe,' James answered doubtfully, as if he couldn't believe anyone would behave like that. 'I suppose you want to go up to Vallance's.'

Of course he did. Down in the basement there he could go into a booth and listen to the latest releases and hear what was new. That was the draw, the music. He'd played guitar since he was thirteen, an old instrument one of his aunts had passed on when she saw how he liked what he heard on the radio. He learned to play it properly, the lessons his father insisted on, hours of practising scales and classical pieces, and enough theory to understand how songs were put together.

And once he realised how simple it all was, pop music had bored him. Until the Beatles came along. With three singles they'd made him realise there was more to it than he'd ever imagined. He'd bought them all, worked out the chords and listened to the way the voices all blended together. It was a new world. And he wanted to step into it.

Once he was working he'd be able to save money for an amplifier and an electric guitar. A Burns, like Hank Marvin played in the Shadows. He'd find a few others who loved the new music and form a group. Give it a little time and they'd be able to play youth club dances. Church halls. And if things went really well there was always the Mecca. After that… well, it would be fun, if nothing else. His dad would hate it, but by now he was used to that. He couldn't live his father's life.

He picked out three singles, the Saturday girl with the beehive hair and tight skirt telling him to go to booth four. He and James were cramped inside, but then the music began and he was lost, listening to the lines the guitars played and the power of the drums. Beat music, they called it, and the term was right. It needed the beat to work properly. James looked bored, but ten minutes later it was over. Chris was smiling as they walked out into the sun on the Headrow.

In the end they simply went and caught the bus home, the long pull up Chapeltown Road. James was itching to go, to put in more time revising for his O-levels, as if he didn't do enough already. They were the only people on the top deck, the windows wide to catch the breeze. They were sitting right at the front, the best seats, where overhanging branches would hit against the glass as if they might break it.

James stared straight ahead, lost in one thought or another. Chris gazed out of the window. The street was full of dark faces. West Indians. A few white people remained, passing through the crowds like fading ghosts. The business signs were colourful, each one offering a mystery. It was a different world. A dangerous one, his father said. But the world was full of fear, according to him. It seemed strange when the man had fought in Burma during the war. What could be so fearful about England?

Soon enough he'd be home. The usual Saturday summer dinner, ham, lettuce and tomato with salad cream. He knew he should spend the afternoon revising, trying to make some sense of calculus. He'd try. He always tried, until it defeated him and he'd put the book away in frustration and pick up his guitar. That always made sense, the logic of chords and notes.

Another month and he'd be washing the ink from his fingers for the last time. He'd hand in his books and walk out of school, take off the tie. Then life could begin. Sometimes he believed that he'd spent all his life just holding his breath, waiting for something to happen.

The bus juddered to a stop across from the war memorial in Chapel Allerton. Wreaths of paper poppies laid in the two minutes of silence last November still stood against it, their blood colour faded to pink by the weather.

He hadn't even been born in 1945. He could only faintly remember the very end of rationing. But so many of his father's generation still lived in that time, as if the fighting had never ended. He'd heard their evening conversations over a bottle of whisky, the longing reminiscences of their finest years, when they were allowed to be real men.

He stood.

'I'll see you on Monday,' he told James, receiving a nod in reply. At the bottom of the stairs the conductor rang the bell. Chris jumped off before the bus stopped moving, almost stumbling until he found his feet.

A new England, he thought as he walked away. That was what they needed.

Historical Note: In 1963 England went boom as youth began to sweep away the older order. Fashion, hairstyles and above all, music, exploded – at least in London, and the myth of the capital as the swinging city of the Sixties was born. Much of that is true. But it took a long time for the reverberations to reach Leeds, still the place of *Billy Liar* and the Victorian values (those imposed by the people with money, that is) that had shaped Leeds since it had become a city in 1895. But eventually those ripples arrived and everything changed…

Available from Armley Press

Coming Out as a Bowie Fan in Leeds, Yorkshire, England
By Mick McCann
ISBN 0-9554699-0-2

Hot Knife
By John Lake
ISBN 0-9554699-1-0

Nailed – Digital Stalking in Leeds, Yorkshire, England
By Mick McCann
ISBN 0-955469-2-9

How Leeds Changed the World – Encyclopaedia Leeds
By Mick McCann
ISBN 0-955469-3-0

Blowback
By John Lake
ISBN 0-9554699-4-7

Speedbomb
By John Lake
ISBN 0-9554699-5-4

In All Beginnings
By Ray Brown
ISBN 0-9554699-6-1

Lightning Source UK Ltd.
Milton Keynes UK
UKHW010756190619
344674UK00001B/228/P

9 780955 469978